Tulasi Acharya
Jan 20, 2024

1

Running from the Dreamland

First Publisher: Allwrite Publishing, P.O. Box 1071 Atlanta Georgia 30301 USA

Learn more about the author at *www.tulasiacharya.com*

Dedication
To Dhan, Sita, Jagriti, and Angela

Chapter 1: Prologue (Graduation)

The long sleeves of Deepak's graduation gown hangs low off his arms. He adjusts his sleeves as he stands waiting to march into the hall with all the other graduates. He looks around for Melissa, but cannot see her in the crowd. *Where did she go? "Of course I will be there" that is what she had told,* Deepak thought.

The faculty lines up outside, dressed in a variety of gowns and hoods of various colors. A piper plays a variety of Scottish songs while the grads march through lines of faculty who greet them with smiles as they make their way to their seats. The hall is massive, full of people. Family, friends and well-wishers sit in the stands. Some have whistles and many have cameras that keep flashing, momentarily blinding the students as they walk. They march in and then wait for the faculty to proceed. A host of other dignitaries walks in behind the faculty and fills the large stage that faced the audience. A student sings the National Anthem in a big, operatic voice. Once she finishes, everyone is invited to sit as the ceremony begins. Deepak looks around for Melissa again, his eyes travelling everywhere in the hall and beyond, but she is nowhere.

The university president makes a long speech to welcome the guests. Then a variety of other people speaks, culminating in a speech by the CEO of a large business in the area. She speaks to the graduates with high hopes, but she keeps getting the pronunciation of the university's name wrong. People around grimace each time she says the name. She encourages the graduates to give back to the community and to strive to be better people.

She reminds them that they are at the start of great things and have a lot to look forward to. She finishes to a round of furious applause, probably because they want the marching across the stage to begin.

They file out in military precision as their names are pronounced and mispronounced by the various deans; they all shake hands with the president, who gives each of them their diploma, a roll of paper tied with a red ribbon. There are shouts and whoops of joy from the crowd as certain people's names are called. Deepak still scans the crowd keenly for Melissa and imagines her cheering when his name is called. While he does not hear her distinctly, he hears someone clap and cheer immediately as the next person's name was announced.

In a flash, they are marching out the hall after their professors and into the evening light. Elated and dejected simultaneously, Deepak once again looks around for Melissa. Most of the new graduates are posing for photos with family and friends.

He had invited his parents to attend his graduation, but the American Embassy in Kathmandu failed to provide them with US visas. Vanessa and her boyfriend Lucas are not there. They were his roommates when he came to the US at first. They are now not in contact with him after Vanessa left Lucas.

Approaching a couple of classmates, Deepak asks if they have seen Melissa around. *What happened to her? Why is she not at my graduation? Is she okay? How can she miss my graduation? She is the love of my life, my American dream, my future,* Deepak ruminates over the absence of Melissa at his graduation.

After an hour of searching, it is clear she has not come. There is no one to congratulate him. Even if there are many people around, it does not matter to him until Melissa shows up. He leaves the graduation hall dejected and hopes that nothing has happened to her. He calls her and her cell phone goes straight to voice message. He wants to go back and knock on her door, but again balks at that idea. He walks towards a bench under a poplar tree on the premises of the university while many

5

graduates and their families are still clicking photos and celebrating their academic success.

Some of them are taking selfies from different angles while others are throwing their mortarboards up in the air and asking someone to click that moment. All of them look jovial, but Deepak still ponders over Melissa not making it to his graduation.

It is almost 6 P.M. The sun sets in the horizon, a glazed turmeric yellow color. The lights in the university buildings are turned on. Deepak sits on the bench just like that. He is not in the mood to go to his apartment. *Perhaps, Melissa will come. I will wait,* he fumbles. His memories of two years ago surface.

Chapter Two: Atlanta

Two years ago, Deepak landed at the Atlanta airport. A woman was standing in front of him waiting in line at the baggage claim area. Dressed totally in electric blue, her long, strawberry blonde hair framed a perfectly oval face that impassively watched the slowly rotating suitcases. From out of nowhere, a man barged through the gaggle of people standing in line and grabbed her. Deepak guessed it was her boyfriend or husband. It was definitely not her brother. She kissed the man so deeply that Deepak felt it in his bones.

Deepak shifted his bag over his shoulder and looked around to see if the university had sent someone to pick him up. His eyes roamed the airport lobby before noticing a guy and a girl, jointly holding a large piece of yellow paper with his name, "**DEEPAK**," printed in bold, black letters. The guy was probably around six feet tall with blue eyes, gingery blond hair, and pronounced biceps that were proudly on display as he held up the sign. The girl was pretty in a South American kind of way: petite, dark brown eyes, with an olive complexion and ringlets of long, dark hair tied loosely in a ponytail. He was wearing stonewashed light blue jeans and a dark blue t-shirt while she was dressed in a white lace dress that clung to her soft curves. They looked almost too eager, their eyes hunting the throng of passengers. Deepak approached, slightly apprehensive and involuntarily clenched his teeth.

"Hello, I believe you're looking for me," he said, forcing a nervous smile through carefully enunciated words.

"Deepak!" The man grinned, as though they'd known each other forever, and grasped his hand

7

in a firm handshake. He had to bow slightly to greet Deepak. "You look just like your picture. I'm Lucas."

"And I'm Vanessa," a delicate, mellifluous voice chimed in, sounding more like she said *Bah*-nessa. She extended her right hand. "Nice to meet you." A smile enhanced by deep red lipstick escaped her lips and spread to the corners of her eyes. Although waif-like, her ample breasts suddenly bewitched Deepak.

His eyes, with a mind of their own, followed the trail of her cleavage. "Nice to meet you too," Deepak replied.

"Okay, let's get your luggage," Lucas said, clasping Deepak on the shoulder and snapping him back to attention. "What does your luggage look like?"

"Right there. I see it!" Deepak motioned excitedly toward a couple of blue suitcases circling the luggage carousel. After less than a minute with these two, his initial hesitation was already shedding and the excitement of being somewhere new was starting to take root.

Around him streamed people of varying shapes, sizes, and colors; some people in uniforms rushed around with a purpose while others jockeyed silver carts toward and away from the baggage claim area. Some were hurrying up the steps of the escalator to catch, perhaps, their flight, and still others gazed around nonchalantly as if this were their second home. The steady hum of different languages beat in his eardrums. Most people looked bewildered, tired from their flight. Many were intent on reading airport signs. Some laughed, smiled, chatted, and talked on the phone. Some headed toward the departure gate, luggage in hand, or pulled tiny suitcases in a variety of colors, mostly black. Others looked at their boarding passes and half-walked, half-trotted to security checkpoints as they tried to get to their waiting gates.

Together, Lucas and Deepak pulled the luggage off the carousel, and all three of them strolled through shining glass doors into the world that awaited the newly arrived traveler.

"Follow us," Lucas and Vanessa said in unison. He followed, aware that his clothes, which had been new when he started his long journey from Kathmandu, were now crumpled and showed all the wear and tear of his two-day journey in the skies. Like many others at that airport, Deepak was on a quest.

He was after the American dream, i.e. to complete his education with a Master's degree and then get a Ph.D., get a good job, be a good writer, marry a beautiful woman and settle in the U. S., the dreamland.

He continued to dream of making enough money to pay off the huge loan he had taken out to travel to America. He dreamed of buying a bungalow back in Nepal so that his parents could move out of their rented room and onto a plot of land in the hubbub city of Kathmandu, Nepal, which would increase in value and be a safety net in years to come.

He dreamed of building his own home in America, a sprawling house like the ones he had seen in films, and owning a brand new Mercedes. When he let his imagination really run wild, his dream was to become a star in Hollywood. He didn't know how or what he would do, all he knew was that he wanted to be a star. Everyone else in America made it look so easy.

Suddenly, he was flooded with uncertainty wondering if the dream would come true or not, Deepak felt perspiration trickling down his back and settling in a tiny puddle at the base of his spine. He was breathing rapidly; he cleared his throat, gripped the handle of the luggage cart tightly, and tried to control his hummingbird heartbeat.

"The United States of America," he whispered under his breath looking at the architecture of the airport building and the carpeted floor, moving escalators that seemed unreal and unimaginable to him.

As he looked around, all the faces looked unfamiliar. Back at home, he could easily spot the foreigners amongst the sea of Nepalese people, but here they all looked like strangers, like people fallen from a different world. He had seen this cornucopia of people sometimes on television, but to experience it first hand was overwhelming. His eyes glazed over as they filled with wonder at the diversity that came alive in front of his eyes. They were as black as coal. They had large muscles and huge arms, almost the size of his thighs.

They were as white as snow, as if all their blood had been drained. They had green eyes, brown eyes, blond hair, and black hair. He saw a woman in her early 50s walking in a skimpy outfit—a tight t-shirt and a mini-skirt— clothes that Deepak had only seen on young people in films.

Deepak looked like an Indian man, with his dark hair, slight build, and wheat-like complexion, until people started mistaking him as Hispanic as the day went by. There was a large number of Hispanic population in the USA, mostly from Mexico and they looked very similar to people from Nepal in terms of their complexion and the eye color, hair, and build.

A closer inspection revealed Deepak's angular face, complete with a nose that was perhaps a little too big for the space it occupied, a mouth that was well defined and quite plump, and—what he considered to be his most striking feature—his large, coal-black eyes framed by long, almost feminine eyelashes. Deepak continued following Lucas and Vanessa, dragging one of the luggage quietly and contemplatively.

"You okay, man?" Lucas interrupted his thoughts. "How was your journey?"

"I'm fine, thank you," Deepak said quickly, breathing a nervous laugh as he tried to compose himself. "It was great, but I'm tired."

Vanessa and Lucas walked ahead, holding hands and stealing kisses. Deepak felt they were promiscuous because he had never witnessed such kisses right in front of him. His Hindu dogmatic grandmother would have said *people of no shame,* Deepak thought. He trailed behind, watching them exchange kisses and suddenly felt engulfed in a sea of strangeness as he struggled to keep up with his companions.

"Deepak, keep up, buddy," Lucas called back. Lucas sounded different when he said Deepak's name. Perhaps, it was an accent.

"Yes, I'm following," Deepak said picking up his pace.

Once they reached the parking lot, the ceiling opened up. Deepak gazed up at this new world, stars twinkled a welcome as the crescent moon hung heavy over him.

The sky looked exactly the same as it did when Deepak left Nepal two days ago. Deepak, meanwhile, became entranced in the glimmering lights and the tempered roar of engines in the distance as aircraft alternately landed and took off. They looked like strange metallic birds invading the earth, jolting and screeching as they landed or soared upwards.

"Let's put your luggage in the trunk." Lucas opened the trunk of the yellow Honda Civic hatchback, and he helped arrange Deepak's luggage in the cramped space that was already half-filled with various books, tools, and bags. Vanessa and Lucas sat in the front while Deepak settled himself in the back seat, behind Vanessa.

"Deepak, don't forget to fasten your seatbelt," Vanessa gently reminded Deepak, the wonderstruck traveler.

"Yes. Thank you." He fumbled with the metal catch of the belt, found its mate embedded in the corner of the seat, and reunited them. Once again, Deepak heard the sounds of kissing coming from Vanessa and Lucas before the car moved off.

"These two need to rent a room," Deepak whispered stifling his thought as quickly as it surfaced. The staccato strains of a Spanish song circled around in the car. Vanessa drove, accelerating out of the parking lot, and merged into a lane filled with traffic.

Mesmerized by the view from the back seat, Deepak watched skyscrapers pass by as the traffic thinned. A river of vehicles rushed from behind and slipped in the front of them as they entered the highway. One after another, cars merged from different directions onto the freeway. The faster the cars moved, the slower they seemed to move as a group. Five-lanes turned into eight-lanes of red and yellow lights. Deepak was enthralled. More buildings appeared and, as if by magic, vanished. The more he looked, the bigger the buildings seemed to become. For the first time, since he began his journey, he felt small under the towering giants along the skyline.

"Will I really make it in such a big country?" Deepak silently said. "Can I pursue my American dream?"

The cornucopia of car lights was the reminder of one of the greatest Nepali festivals called Tihar, also called the festival of lights. He remembered, during *Tihar*, people lit candles, illuminating the darkness and filling the night sky with the colors and the smell of candle wax. He inhaled sharply as a feeling of homesickness hit him in the pit of his stomach and made his eyes water.

"Hey, are you okay?" Vanessa asked. Without waiting for a reply, she added, as a way to change the conversation, "What program are you enrolled in at Georgia University?" Georgia University had offered him a letter to enroll into the program for which he was able to get a student visa and arrive in the USA.

Through the gap in the center of the car, Deepak could see her right hand caressing Lucas' leg while her other hand deftly controlled the steering wheel.

"Creative writing," he answered more confidently than he felt.

"Oh, nice! I've heard that's a great program."

"I hope so"

"So, what do you plan to do when you graduate?" Vanessa was doing her best to make him feel at ease with small talk.

"I plan to do a Ph.D. and work as a professor at an American university, become a published author, and perhaps do something in films" he finished answering in a single breath. His slumped shoulders rose now in pride.

"You will do it, Deepak," she said, her laugh decorated her voice. "America is the land of opportunity. If you go after it, you can achieve it."

That is exactly what Deepak was thinking of. It was now double confirmed that America was a dreamland and the land of opportunity. He found Vanessa speaking his mind.

"Thank you," he said sincerely. He hadn't realized how much he'd needed her words of comfort until he heard them.

"You look very young to be entering a master's degree program. How old are you?" she asked while driving and gazing on the highway. Deepak blushed and shifted uneasily in his seat. Perhaps, he felt good at her words.

"Really? I finished my first master's degree in Nepal when I was 21," He said as if at a job interview. "I was a lecturer of English literature and journalism. I taught at a few colleges in Nepal, and I have also written a few textbooks. I am fascinated with poetry, words, and the messages they communicate." Deepak answered more than what he was asked for. This was his weakness or funny habit if not it was the manifestation of his pride. Another habit was he talked so fast that he became breathless. While talking, he moved his hands quickly to articulate himself.

"That's great! Awesome! You will do it here, too! You are in America now" Vanessa said. The car was moving like in a race.

Deepak was unsure whether Vanessa understood his English pronunciation clearly, but she was, at least, enthusiastically supportive.

Lucas removed an earphone bud from his left ear, leaned towards Vanessa, and cooed, "Baby, did you say something?"

"Nope, I'm talking to Deepak. Baby, you need to talk to him too!" Vanessa said caressing his fingers with her right hand.

Lucas either didn't hear or care; instead, he kissed Vanessa's hand and put his earphones back in. Lucas' body swayed from side to side

14

rhythmically, and he hummed along to the music in his ear bud.

"So how do you like America so far?" Vanessa asked, making up for Lucas' silence.

"It's amazing," Deepak said, looking out the window. Rather than bore her with traveler's woes, a small smile crossed his lips. "You know what?"

"What's that?" Vanessa said, giving him a quick glance in the back.

"When I was landing, I looked out of the plane's window and thought that the airport parking lot was a car dealership."

"You're funny!" Vanessa laughed.

The car was still in the highway 70 miles per hour. Lucas heard her laughter and removed his earphones. "What happened?"

"*Amor*, Deepak thought that the parking lot at the airport was a car dealership." She laughed again.

"That's classic!" Lucas chuckled, and then teased, "Aren't there such big parking lots in Nepal?"

"No, very few people have cars, so no need to have big parking lots."

"Oh, really?" Lucas' voice betrayed a measure of surprise. "What's Nepal like? It's got a lot of mountains, right?"

"Yes, and it is beautiful — shimmering lakes, snow- clad glittering mountains, and tweeting, chirping and dancing birds. It is full of amazing, beautiful gorges, caves, and springs—they all face the sky as though they mean to receive rain from the heavens."

"Hold up, wait, wait," Lucas lost track of what Deepak was saying in the middle of his description.

"The lakes feel like they extend beyond the

15

horizon," Deepak continued as his hands gesticulated wildly, "and there's always a gentle, cool breeze around them. When the sun shines, water in the lake glitters, turning everything silver and gold. Machhapuchhre Mountain shows its face in the mirror of the Fewa lake; it puts a spell on every visitor, like a giant shark undulating in the lake." Deepak was lost in the images of his homeland, soothing him, spellbound with memories.

"Well, shit! I believe you're a poet, bro!" Lucas laughed, tossing his head backwards. "You're Nepalese William Shakespeare!"

"Believe me, anyone would be overwhelmed by the beauty of Nepal," Deepak said, his voice was sincere if not a little defensive.

"You ever climbed Mount Everest?" Lucas asked. This was the same question Deepak was frequently asked when he met a new person in the US. Many of them didn't even know Mount Everest lies in Nepal. "Oh really, I thought it was in China or India?" was a surprise response when Deepak told them the truth that Mount Everest is in Nepal.

"No."

"But Mount Everest is in Nepal, right?"

"Yes, but it is not easy to climb, you know?" Deepak continued. "You need to go through extensive mountaineering training before you can even begin to climb Mount Everest."

Lucas gave a small, meaningless grunt then went back to his headphones while Vanessa continued driving. They passed small towns, still big building and skyscrapers, wide roads, traffic lights, strip malls and others that did not look very clear as it was already evening, but they glimmered under the street lights.

They finally arrived at a large apartment complex cluttered with trees. The apartment gate displayed the name of the apartment complex with the

16

letter "GREENHOUSE APARTMENT." It was dark, but Deepak could still make out what looked like hundreds of parked cars in uniform rows. This was where Vanessa and Lucas lived, and the place Deepak was to call his new home.

Chapter 3: The Apartment

"We've been here for a few months, and so far, we can't complain. The university is just ten minutes away. This is your room," Lucas gestured, showing Deepak a middle- sized section squared off from the living room. It was painted a non-descript beige color. A large, white ceiling fan hung in the center of the room, and a number of white doors lead to other rooms and closets. He motioned to a corner of the room, sparsely furnished with a small grey sofa, an oblong light wooden table, and a couple of white, plastic chairs. "We can probably separate it for you if you want."

"It's okay. This is fine," Deepak said, hoping his voice did not betray his disappointment.

"Let's order pizza," Vanessa chimed in. "Deepak must be hungry."

"I would like to take a shower first," Deepak said looking around. "Where is the bathroom?" They showed him the bathroom just the opposite of their bedroom.

After showering and donning a clean t-shirt and shorts, he rejoined Vanessa and Lucas. The pizza had already arrived. Deepak never had seen pizza in his entire life, let alone eating them. Perhaps they were served in Kathmandu in five star hotels or any sophisticated restaurants where he never went, nor could he afford to visit based on the salary he earned from his teaching job. He saw the pizza's slices enormous and dripping with cheese.

"Wow, very large piece!" Deepak said, taking a bite of it and thanking them for it. "Look yummy." He also took a bite of it, but didn't like it right away and continued to hold it just to make sure that they would not think he disrespected the food they offered. But he found them craving for it while they ate it. Deepak realized likes or dislikes of things depended on one's habituation or the cultivation of the habit toward it.

They started talking about the apartment over the bites of the pizza slices.

"We have been paying $600 plus utilities per month," Lucas said between bites. "I figure you can just pay $300 a month including utilities. Just try to keep the kitchen and the bathroom clean. Does that sound right?"

"That's fine," Deepak said although it was a little too much for him.

Deepak looked around the room once again. The living room was a mess. Books were scattered on the floor and unwashed dishes were left in the sink. A dilapidated red bicycle was abandoned in the corner near the front door, and a trickle of black grease oozed from the bike chain, leaving an oily stain on the carpet. Half a dozen black and white kittens mewed beside their mother. Deepak covered his nose secretly as if he were picking it. Perhaps, the acrid smell of urine burned the inside of his nose. A litter tray was in the corner of the room near the cats, filled with gray gravel and the lumps of feces.

At first, Deepak became furious internally as he wondered how he could live in such a filthy living room. The cleanliness of the room stood just the opposite of what he had pictured before he ventured to the US—neat and clean and tidy, filled with fragrance and absolutely different ambience from the type of apartment he lived in while in Kathmandu. *Yes, room doesn't look as wonderful and spacious as here, but the room I lived back in Kathmandu was way tidier than this,* Deepak quickly thought. He knew that, no matter what, he should be grateful that they were allowing him to stay with them at all, but the place was not what he had expected in the land of dreams.

"What do you think?" Lucas asked. "If you need a bike, you can fix that one up and use it." He pointed toward the bicycle in the corner of the living room.

"Great," Deepak said with forced enthusiasm. "It's fine, such a nice place!" He tried to sound congenial and hoped that they didn't sense how unhappy he was with the room.

"What are you two studying?" Deepak asked in an attempt to change the subject.

Lucas took Vanessa, still with a piece of the pizza in their hands, gently in his arms. "My little bunny is a nursing major, and I'm a business major. We're both undergrads."

"We're like a mini United Nations here," Vanessa giggled, squinting up at Lucas.

"Are you married?" Deepak asked boldly. They blinked back at him in surprise.

"Not yet, but soon," Vanessa responded a little too quickly. They were living together for two years or so.

A kitten mewed, breaking into their conversation.

"Why do you have so many cats?" Deepak asked with a surprise, looking at the playing kittens.

"Lucas is a cat lover," Vanessa responded, as she reached down and picked a kitten up by the scruff of its neck and began massaging its back, while she still had a piece of pizza in her hand.

"Not really. Actually, we had only one cat. She went outside and had sex, and this is the result," Lucas retorted immediately, guffawing. Deepak chuckled at Lucas's answer. Vanessa also chuckled, blushing bright red.

"Maybe Deepak wants to sleep. He must be tired; you know how awful jetlag is," Vanessa said looking at Lucas and collecting the pizza box. "Let him sleep, *Amor!*"

"I'm a little tired, but that's okay," Deepak said yawning, his eyes involuntarily filled with water. He was tired, but, at the same time, he was filled with awe and wonder. He was anxious too as it was his first day in the United States of America surrounded by new people as his friends and roommates.

Vanessa unhinged herself from Lucas' grasp, trashing the pizza box and walked to her bedroom. She returned, tugging a blue and white quilt and pillow. "Take these. You can use them until you can buy your own," She said, folding the sofa out into a bed. Vanessa showed him how it worked, pointed to her laptop by the sofa and told him "you can use it. I have another laptop too," and then the two bid him goodnight and slipped off behind the white door into their bedroom.

"Thank you so much," Deepak said.

Deepak trashed the pizza slice in his hand into the nearby bin because he didn't find its taste as delicious as it looked after they left him. Deepak unfolded the quilt, spread it across the sofa, and settled down, feeling much like a stranger who was passing the night in a hillside inn in Nepal. He spotted a cockroach scurrying across the floor looking for crumbs.

Deepak closed his eyes and tried to sleep, but sleeping in the living room left him feeling exposed. He fumed inwardly that he had to pay $300 per month to sleep on a couch! He tried to reconcile the seeming injustice of the situation. He wondered if he could rent a room on his own soon. In his heart, Deepak knew that this wouldn't be as easy as he hoped. The realization began to dawn that his dreams might not be as easy to fulfill as he had thought.

Deepak did not sleep well. Thoughts circled around in his head. He remembered his family, his friends, and everyone that had come to see him off in Nepal.

All his relatives gathered at the family house on the eve of his flight to America. His parents cried tears of joy. His sisters' cheeks bloomed like proud orchids, and his relatives were amazed that Deepak got a U.S. visa.

Some gossiped, saying "Deepak is going to buy a five-story mansion from the dollars he will earn in America!"

"You are going to make your fortune!" one said. "Congratulations, Deepak!" another added.

His eyes welled up again and his tears dampened the pillow while he thought of the American dream he was on a mission to pursue. The tears were more than for missing home, i.e. he finally made it to America. He wiped his face on the quilt and thought to himself that he had to lose many things to gain something important in his life, such as family and homeland and live with memories in a foreign land.

The sofa was not comfortable. Deepak spread the bedcover on the floor instead and lay down on his back. He tossed and turned on the hard floor that the quilt did not soften. Closing his eyes, he still could not sleep. The newness of everything was overwhelming. Different feelings played hide and seek in his head; he imagined what his future life would be like. He spread his dreams out in front of him and did the math to try to estimate how many of them would be fulfilled. Silence filled the air. It seemed that everybody around him was soundly asleep. The world was sleeping. It was a different and uncharted world. Light streamed through from the outside. He tossed and turned over the bed. It was already morning.

Through the window, the sunlight danced in the room sending some rays on the laptop Vanessa had told him he could use. Deepak grabbed the laptop from the table and was able, with a little perseverance, to get online and read his emails. He found ten messages in his inbox; most of them were from his friends back home. All the emails seemed to say, "Are you okay? Did you arrive in the USA? We miss you, Deepak." He could imagine his friends writing emails to him at dusty Internet shops in between the daily power cuts and load shedding that the Nepalese experienced as a way of life. His nose began to burn; his eyes blurred. In his mind's eye, he saw his sister crying at the airport and his parents' lachrymose tone as they wished him the best.

He could not control his feelings. His eyes again watered and tears hit the laptop, perhaps the mixed feelings of both pain and pleasure. He could not read the emails anymore. All the letters on the screen blurred into a congealed mess. He wiped his face with his hands, but again tears rolled down by themselves. Like a small child, he cried but silently. He hiccupped. His mother used to tell him if he hiccupped that meant someone dearest would remember him. He wondered if his parents or sister thought about him.

He looked outside the window. The sunlight was coming straight from it, blurring his vision to look further and beyond. He saw some trees that he would not know the names of and cars parked.

The sound of footsteps alerted him that someone had surfaced from the bedroom. He looked up quickly to see a tousled-haired Lucas framed in the harsh morning light.

"Hey, Deepak. Good Morning!" Lucas said. "How was your sleep?"

"Yes, it was fine, Lucas. Thank you, I was just thinking of my parents back home," Deepak answered quickly.

"Things happen when you leave your family first time," Lucas said running the tap in the kitchen. "You gotta be brave, man."

It's okay. I am good," said Deepak, forcing a smile.

Deepak got up and went to the bathroom. His swollen and tired eyes looked back at him in the mirror. He left the bathroom and stepped into the kitchen, where he could smell Lucas cooking something.

Deepak felt his stomach grumble. "Oh, that's a nice smell. What's that?"

"If you are hungry, you can have some. Vanessa loves this stuff."

"You love your girlfriend very much, huh?" Deepak said as he settled in at the table.

"Oh, yeah," Lucas started putting food on his plate. "You want some? Feel free to have one."

"What is it?" Deepak said, getting up from the chair and approaching Lucas to take a look at what he offered him to eat.

"It's a steak burger. Do you eat beef?"

"Oh, hell no!" Deepak said, his eyes opened wide and an involuntary scowl crossed his face.

"I take that as a no," Lucas added hesitantly.

"No, I cannot even imagine eating beef. The cow is holy in our religion. She represents the goddess Laxmi, the goddess of wealth in the Hindu religion, so to eat beef is to have committed a great sin, an unpardonable sin."

"Oh, really? Shit." Lucas frowned

24

apologetically, "I am so sorry, man. I didn't know."

"It's okay. No problem. Culture is a bitch, I guess," Deepak said.

Lucas walked back toward their bedroom with the plate of beef in his hand, saying, "Sure. You know, you can just help yourself to something. You're not a guest. You live here."

"I will. Thank you," Deepak said coming back to the sofa.

The bedroom door clicked shut behind Lucas and Deepak got up from the sofa and again began to scrounge through the kitchen for something to cook. He found a bag of red potatoes in the refrigerator. He remembered his sister cooked rice for him in the morning and brought it to him in bed. His mother cooked cauliflower curry in the kitchen and served him. At home, Deepak only entered the kitchen to smell the spicy food his mother had made.

Again, he thought of himself doing all those kitchen chores when he started renting a room in Kathmandu and lived there for eight years until he left for America. He tried to put the potatoes back, but they slipped out of his hand and fell to the floor with a bang. Potatoes scattered in all directions. He quickly picked up the vegetables and decided to make a potato curry. Feeling a little more secure, he cut the potatoes into even cubes and fried them in a pan. He pictured his apartment life while in Kathmandu—cooking, eating, washing and cleaning, going to college, teaching and the like.

He hadn't informed his parents about his arrival. He asked Vanessa if there was a way he could talk to his parents back home to let them know that he had arrived safely.

"Oh, you can use my phone. I always use calling cards to call my parents back home in Peru," Vanessa said. "I have some cards here; you can use one." Vanessa dialed the number for him and helped him connect to his parents.

"*Buwa*, don't worry. I have safely arrived here. My roommates are wonderful and they are helping me a lot," he said.

After a few minutes of conversation, he felt relieved and thought of the American dream ahead.

Chapter 4: The University

It was drizzling outside, thunder rolling in the distance, when Lucas offered to take Deepak on a tour through campus before classes would start on the 14th of August. Deepak agreed, and Lucas, seemingly excited about showing someone around, grabbed an umbrella and shoved it in Deepak's hands. Once outside, Deepak opened the umbrella and asked Lucas to come under it.

"I don't need the umbrella, man. The rain is good for you," Lucas said. "It's not gonna make me wet."

"You might catch a cold!"

"Hey, don't worry about me. I love rain."

They walked downhill for about half a mile before turning to the left, where they continued walking until a busy intersection welcomed them to the outskirts of the university campus.

The poplar trees with their verdant color leaves stood on either side of the road and squirrels scurried up the trees. The drizzling lessened to a light drizzle as they navigated through the red brick buildings on the university campus. Lucas pointed out the buildings that housed academic programs— the tennis court, the theatre hall, and the recreation center. They all looked the same and Deepak had to remind himself that once he was taking classes here, he would get the hang of it. They entered the cafeteria and Deepak shook off his umbrella.

"This is the heart of the university," Lucas said. "Can we get coffee? I am parched."

They bought two cups of coffee and sat by the window where Deepak could see the last drops of rain coming down. The place was a rectangle, with long aisles separating tables in scattered uniformity. The tables were a dirty cream color and the chairs, a metallic black. The cafeteria was huge, both sides lined with mini individual food franchises. He could spot a Chinese food station, a pizza station, a comfort food station with burgers and fries, and various baked sweets. People, perhaps working for the university, lined up at the stations and sat at the tables in gaggles, laughing like old friends. The classes had not started, but the administrative work was underway.

"Our cafeteria is so big. You wouldn't think the university is actually dirt cheap," Lucas said as he lifted his cup of the coffee and sipped it. Deepak had never seen such as big cafeteria in the university. One of the biggest universities he went to in Nepal was Tribhuvan University and the cafeteria of it was not even a one third of what he saw here. Back in Nepal, there were stalls of cafeteria almost one per department.

"Indeed, it is really big, wide and spacious," Deepak said with a sip of coffee, "By the way, how much do you pay a year?"

"You mean the tuition fee?" Lucas said over a cup of coffee as he lifted it.

"Yes," Deepak said.

"Six thousand per semester."

"That's a lot of money,"

"Yes, but I don't have to pay. The Swedish government does!" Lucas looked smugly at his companion and asked, "how about you?"

"I," he grimaced, as if strange feelings of panic made his stomach go into spasms. "I wish I was in your place; I have to work."

"Can you work off campus legally if you're on a student visa and not a US citizen?" Lucas asked, dropping his voice and with his eyebrows up.

"That's the biggest challenge I am going to face," Deepak said. The words seemed to stick in his mouth, which had instantly become very dry. He knew he was not legally allowed to work off campus, but there was no way he could finance his education and realize his dreams otherwise. Before arriving in America, he had

28

general visions of what his life would be like after "making it." Now that he had been in the country and witnessed, first hand, the lifestyle possibilities for himself, the urgency had gotten greater and the visions became more specific. He thought he needed to make his American dream come true.

"Perhaps I can find some Asian stores," Deepak said.

"Why Asian stores?" Lucas' eyebrows rose in surprise, with the coffee up in his hand.

"Because I have heard that they might, at least, hire people like me. Low pay, though." Deepak knew it was very risky, but he felt he had no other way to finance his education. Reluctantly, he admitted, "My family back home is poor, and they cannot support me. I had to support my parents while in Nepal and I did so by teaching at a few colleges in Kathmandu. My parents still live in the countryside working on the farm and making a meager income"

"That's rough, man. Good luck though, dude." Lucas said, finishing his coffee. The cream left a tiny moustache on his upper lip. "But you need to be careful," he added lowering his voice. "If you are found working illegally, you will be deported. You know that, don't you?"

"I know, I know, but what can I do?" Deepak continued to stare at his feet.

"Listen, you better go and see the director of the International Admissions Office to see if they can help you sort out your financial situation. You never know."

Shame engulfed Deepak, and he felt the tips of his ears burning. He could not find the right words to respond, so he finished his coffee instead and threw the cup into the trashcan.

"Let's head back before the rain starts up again," Lucas said, and Deepak welcomed the invitation. In a somber mood, the two got up and left the campus.

29

At the apartment, Vanessa was in the kitchen washing dishes. Lucas grabbed her from behind and flipped her around to kiss her. "How are you, baby?" That question came into play frequently even if they reunited after a few minutes. *Perhaps American culture*, Deepak thought silently.

Deepak heard Vanessa laugh, squealing playfully against his wet clothes but turning and kissing Lucas back all the same. Vanessa's white top didn't stand up well against Lucas' wet shirt, and Deepak caught a glimpse of the dark pink areola of her breast underneath. He quickly averted his eyes, turning to look out the window. Lucas was rubbing her back, his hand under her shirt, murmuring something softly to her.

The rain had completely abated, and, outside the window, the sky looked clear although a thin layer of clouds hovered overhead. The wind was strong enough for Deepak to hear the leaves of the poplar trees rustling. The conversation of tuition fee with Lucas weighed heavily on his mind. It dawned on him that dreams did not just happen; he needed to work hard for them to become reality. Still, he was not looking forward to the hard journey ahead of him.

Lucas finally peeled himself off of Vanessa. She pulled a sweater over her head when she noticed Deepak staring out the window morosely.

"What's the matter, Deepak?" Vanessa asked, settling in beside him. She seemed to know his moods. "You look sad and tired."

"I'm alright, Vanessa," Deepak answered, his smile was little more than a grimace.

"Are you gonna register for your classes?" Lucas slipped behind Vanessa to massage her shoulders, his top lip raised in the tiniest of smirks.

"Not yet. I need a job. I don't have all the money to pay right away for early registration." Deepak's expression on his face shifted downward. Deepak had brought $1500 with him and the first semester fee was $3000. On top of that, he had to pay the rent and buy food and other miscellaneous items. There were other responsibilities, such as paying the $1500 loan back home and supporting his parents.

"If you don't have money, how did you show the college your bank statement before they issued an I20?" Lucas challenged. I20 was a paper document along with an offer letter from the university stating the student's ability to finance the education in the US.

"It was a fake bank statement. I had to bribe someone for $100, my friend!"

"You're too funny!" Lucas laughed, perhaps thinking that it was just ridiculous. Deepak smiled wryly.

"Do you know if there are any Nepali people living around here?" Deepak's voice cracked as he spoke.

Vanessa did her best to put him at ease. "I don't know, maybe!"

Lucas chimed in, "Maybe they'd help you, Deepak. I'll keep an eye out."

"Be brave, Deepak!" Vanessa gave him a smile. "We're all international students. It's not easy here. You've got to struggle." She motioned with her hand. "When I came to the US, I came as a nanny, and now I'm in the nursing program. One day, you'll make your living. You'll be fine."

"Thanks, Vanessa," Deepak said, hoping her promises would come to fruition. The first two weeks seemingly flew by. Deepak spent his time getting accustomed to the apartment and venturing outside to nearby shopping centers and the like. In one local store, he found a supply of cumin, turmeric, and coriander seeds, and his cooking improved noticeably with their addition to his meals. Nepalese food, a combination of Chinese and Indian cuisine, is often spicy and flavorful, which caught Vanessa's interest on one occasion. Although she asked Deepak a few questions about the origin and preparation of *Dal,* she refused to try the rich bean soup. "I'll just wait until Lucas gets home, and we'll probably just grab a burger," she said in response to Deepak's offer to "try some."

He was ready to go to college the next day. It was going to be his first day in class, first time at a US university.

Chapter 5: Challenges

Next day, Deepak woke up as the weak sunlight streamed through the window of his sectioned-off area of the room. The dust particles in the beams of light danced up and down and, for a second, Deepak forgot his situation. Soon, however, reality forced its way into his consciousness, and his head was suddenly heavy with the burden of his financial challenges. Early registration came and went, and he'd finally been able to sign up for his classes. Now, the next day to pay his tuition fee was quickly approaching. He needed to pay $3,000 by the end of this month, but he only had half of that. *I wouldn't be able to pay tuition until I find a job,* he fumbled over and over again by the thought of the tuition fee. He looked out the window toward the east where the sun was rising. The birds were leaving their homes and flying across the sky, maybe beginning to make their long, arduous journey to warmer climates, as the winter was approaching.

Deepak ate breakfast and went to campus early, several hours before his classes started at 10 a.m. At first he thought of what Lucas suggested that he should speak with the director of the International Admission Office. But he decided to, at first, stop at the English department to talk to Professor Jack Williams, the director of his program. *There might be a possibility of a student assistant position,* he thought silently. If his professor could give him a student assistant position, his immediate financial problems would be better, and it could mean a steady source of income.

Professor Williams was sitting in his office, fingers clicking over his laptop. He looked so busy that he would not notice anyone coming by until someone would knock on his door.

Deepak glanced around the office. On the wall

hung large certificates—a Ph.D. from UCLA and a myriad of other documents that spoke to his intellectual prowess. Dark brown shelves were filled with many books, such as anthologies of poetry, short stories, and a number of books about homosexuality. Deepak guessed Professor Williams might be gay, but he could not be sure. In Nepal, gay people rarely held positions of power. Gays, women, children, disabled were always marginalized. Deepak shrugged the thought aside when the professor glanced up at him expectantly from under his glasses.

"May I help you?" Professor Williams said, looking at Deepak as if he was spying.

"Hello, sir, my name is Deepak, coming from Nepal, new international student in your program?" Deepak asked him from the doorway. It was Deepak's first meeting with the professor Williams.

"Oh, wow, Deepak, come on in," he said, gesturing Deepak to the chair in front of his desk. Deepak quickly took a seat, no doubt looking as anxious as he felt because Professor Williams' next question was, "It is great to meet you. How are you?"

"I am fine, Sir, how are you?"

"Good, good," Williams showed interest in him. "What's the matter?" His attitude appeared feminine in terms of his bodily movements and gesticulations.

"Sir, I am in financial difficulties," he said, voice trembling. "Can you do something to provide a research assistantship for me?"

Deepak's question for Williams felt ridiculous. Deepak was just coming to see him for the first time and bringing his financial problems. That appeared to be funny to Professor Williams. All of a sudden, he seemed to be losing any interest in continuing the conversation with Deepak.

"Look, Deepak, I am just meeting with you. You have not even started the first semester and you say this,"

Professor Williams said. "I can't do anything about this." Professor Williams said in a monotonous voice as if repeating a tired old story. He removed his glasses and put them on the table. "I have no authority to provide a research assistantship for you. The professors in the department must personally decide after reviewing your resume." He looked irritated, but Deepak didn't leave the chair he was sitting in.

"Sir, I have lengthy experience in writing, research, and teaching while in Nepal. I also have authored a few books. Can I not get any kind of assistantship relevant to my area of knowledge?" Deepak insisted. He knew being persistent was not always a desirable trait, but he had found that it did not hurt to ask. It also could be part of Nepali culture that mentored him to be pushy to obtain what he wanted. Perhaps the culture he was brought up in taught him that persistence was a key to success.

Deepak remembered what his mother had said, "genius is 1% inspiration, 99% perspiration." A trickle of sweat rolled down the side of his face.

"At this moment, I can't say anything," Professor William spoke firmly.

"Sir, can't you do anything on my behalf? If my financial problems ease, I can then concentrate on my studies," Deepak continued to ask hopefully.

"You can try the library. Sometimes they hire students. You might get a chance in any department. Please, go there, and let them know what you are looking for," William said before putting the glasses back on and looking at the computer screen.

"I asked the other departments, sir, but to no avail," Deepak to some extent lied hoping professor Williams would sympathize with his situation. He squirmed inwardly and his cheeks flushed red.

"Let me tell you the truth, Deepak. I can't do anything for you other than to suggest that you go home if you can't pay the tuition fee or if you cannot get a job on campus. I can't give you money from my pocket." Professor Williams spoke quickly. That was the strongest statement he ever made. Deepak had to listen intently to take everything in. "Before we offered you an I20, we confirmed with you if you could pay the tuition fee." Deepak could not say it was a fake document he made. Professor William's statement hit him so hard that he immediately thought of his American dream. *No I cannot go back to Nepal,* Deepak fumed and objected inwardly.

"My desire is not to go home, sir, but to study very hard and become successful," Deepak found himself repeating words as if a character in a play. He realized it would be useless to continue talking to Williams about his financial problems. He hesitated before relenting. "Okay, sir, I will try to look for a job in the library. Thank you." He turned to leave Professor Williams' office without even noticing that he had been unofficially dismissed about five minutes prior.

Deepak came out of the building. He saw a few students scattered on the ground. His eyes fell on everybody around him; they were familiarly unfamiliar to him. Girls walked in groups, wearing mini-skirts that showed off their sexy, provocative legs. Some girls were dressed in tight dresses, revealing every curve of their bodies. Their asses rose with each step, and their breasts looked like a couple of pigeons ready to fly. The brightly colored Saris and body disguising *Kurtas* and *Suruwal* that women wore in Nepal seemed like distant memories now. Boyfriends and girlfriends kissed here. Girlfriends slumbered on their boyfriends' laps. His eyes fixated on a pair smoking and playing with the smoke that they puffed out in ring shapes. He looked at the smoke from those cigarettes morosely.

A variety of terrifying scenarios haunted him. *How can I make the American dream come true if I cannot pay the tuition fee? How could I maintain a good GPA if I have to work all the time? How could I study well? How could I buy the textbooks? Go home! Go home! Go back to your own country!*, these questions and thoughts continuously haunted him. *If I go back to Nepal, how could I help my parents? When and how could I pay the interest on the loan I have taken out before coming to America? What would those neighbors say who thought I was the luckiest person to get a US visa? What would be the privileged status of my parents because of me being in America? Oh, God help me!* Deepak yelled inwardly.

Deepak had his first class today. All the evening classes began at 6 P.M. He strolled around, explored the university, the buildings and the library. The trees were waiting for foliage as fall had started. Since it was the first day of the fall semester, the college was crowded with students. He entered the library and picked up a free newspaper The New York Times. He thought he had also worked for a national daily newspaper while in Nepal. He had also wanted to work for CNN one day. *The headquarters of CNN is in Atlanta, not far from here*, he ruminated with the newspaper in his hand. He flipped through the pages and glanced over the opinionated page that he always liked to read. He looked around the library, found it neat and clean, and decorated with books. It was very spacious and fully carpeted— red with blue polka dots, the color Deepak liked. A clock hanging against the wall of the library hit 6 P.M.

Deepak entered the classroom for his first lesson, and he felt empty. There were around 10 students sitting in chairs with attached mini-tables where they could put their books and notebooks. Deepak also found a chair next to a student in her mid-twenties. The professor was a woman in her mid-40s, dressed in a deep red pantsuit. She started to explain the syllabus but failed to provide a hard copy. Finally, Deepak, who was having trouble keeping up, raised his hand.

"It would be much easier if you could provide us with a hard copy of the syllabus," Deepak said. All his classmates looked at him as though he had grown a third eye. His accent was thick, and he realized it was difficult for them to understand his words. His professor also asked him to repeat what he had said.

"Speak slowly, please," his professor asked.

"Do you have a hard copy of your syllabus?" he repeated slowly. Deepak became nervous. He was an English teacher in Kathmandu and everyone back home spoke highly of his English, but here they seemed to be snickering at his accent and English, Deepak wondered.

Still, no one seemed to understand what Deepak was talking about and stared at him blankly. The girl seated next to him, however, offered a guess. "Are you asking for a hard copy of the syllabus?" Oh, she is pretty, Deepak whispered silently. She had blue eyes in blue outfit; she had blonde hair and a smile of kindness.

"Yes," Deepak nodded, relieved that someone finally understood him.

"You can look up the syllabus on Blackboard," the she said, speaking slowly, as if mimicking him.

"What is that *Blackboard*?" Deepak asked. "I have never heard of it." In his head, he pictured something he had in the classroom and wrote on with chalk.

"I'll explain it to you later," she whispered and then offered a smile. "By the way, my name is Melissa." She extended her hand to shake with Deepak's. He felt the softness of her hand and its warmth.

He smiled back at her, but inwardly, he was horrified. He again thought, *back in Nepal, people complimented me on my English. Here, they couldn't understand a word I said.* His grandmother referred to English as *gai khane bhasha,* meaning the language spoken by people who eat beef. Deepak swore in silence and became mad at himself. *My accent is terrible! How can I be a professor of English if no one can understand me?* he murmured.

After class, Melissa showed him how Blackboard worked on her laptop even after all the classmates left the room. And they together headed toward the student parking lot.

"Thank you for your help today," Deepak said.

"My pleasure," she responded.

They chatted as they walked. He told her a little about himself, and she seemed genuinely interested. Melissa was of Irish ancestry. Originally from Texas and with a bit of a Southern accent, she explained that she was pursuing a master's degree in English with a major in Creative Writing that Deepak was majoring in too. Again, her topaz blue eyes, dirty blonde hair, cherry red lips and cute smile pulled at the strings of his heart. After they reached the parking deck, Melissa asked Deepak, "Can I drive you to your apartment?" Deepak was not very sure if it was okay to say "yes". He was used to being insisted on in the culture he was grown up so he said "no, thank you," but Melissa didn't insist. Perhaps she thought that would be rude. Deepak later discovered that was kind of an American way.

Still reeling from their brief conversation, Deepak looked back at her as she walked away. She smiled and waved once she noticed him staring as she slid behind the wheel of a bright orange Volkswagen Beetle.

Back at his apartment without Melissa to distract him, his humiliating experience in the English classroom dwelled in the forefront of his mind. He threw his backpack on the sofa in disgust and rushed into the kitchen to find something to relieve his hunger since the cafeteria was too expensive. He spoke his frustrations aloud, swearing in Nepali. *I did not even understand the accent of this janthi professor, these Kuires and whites.* In a fit of rage, he stamped his foot on the floor like a small child throwing a tantrum.

Routine had set in. He cooked rice, potatoes and

bitter gourd curry. While mumbling, the knife slipped as he cut up the bitter gourd. His middle finger became a victim of his temper and bled. He washed his finger, but by now his appetite had vanished and he could do nothing but stare at the finished meal. It reminded him of time spent with his parents and siblings eating rice in the kitchen at home. His eyes burned and welled up. He closed them hard enough to stop the flow of tears and forced the food he had cooked into his dry mouth.

He went to the sofa with a restless mind. While tossing in the sofa, he decided to take up Lucas' suggestion to visit the director of the International Student Office and throw himself at his mercy if he would find a way to pay the tuition fee or any on-campus job. After reconciling this decision, Deepak slept a little more soundly.

Chapter 6: Job Hunt

Deepak wrung his hands together while waiting outside the door of the International Admission Office, trying to gather up courage to go inside. Another student walked into the hallway and sat down across from him.

"Nervous?" the person asked. Deepak glanced up, blinking in surprise when he saw the student across from him smiling back at him. "Don't worry, whatever your problems are, they can't be as bad as mine."

"What did you do?" Deepak asked curiously, matching the other person's boldness.

The student just kept grinning.

"I used a fake bank statement to get in here. Crazy, huh?" he said quietly, with a confidence as if Deepak also could have done exactly the same.

"Me too," Deepak felt his expression go blank with a surprise. Deepak thought he found his mate.

"David," he said introducing himself to Deepak and shaking hands with him.

"I am Deepak" he said. "Nice to meet you."

While waiting for Bulkio to be free and call the next student in line, they already became friends and exchanged their phone numbers. Deepak realized how in a foreign land people looked for something in common between differences and created bonds that could hardly be a practice in his own country.

At that moment, the door opened up and a renewed sense of foreboding swept over Deepak. "You better not keep him waiting," David encouraged softly. Clearly, he had been in Deepak's shoes before. Deepak nodded in gratitude as he approached the door bearing a sign that read: *Bulkio, Director of ISA.*

"Can I help you?" Bulkio's accent - a deep, Bulgarian accent - was new to Deepak. He was no more

41

than 5'6" with a large mustache and a shaved head. He was clad in a starched khaki jacket and tailored navy pants. He had two computers in front of him and looked from one to the other often, only occasionally glancing up at his visitor.

"Yes, sir," Deepak said, as he stood at the door. Bulkio did not speak or motion for him to come in. He remained at the door a little longer before hesitantly entering the room and gingerly sitting in a chair nearest to the door.

"What can I do for you?" Bulkio said. His tiny blue elephant like eyes were not welcoming, even as they flitted from the computer to Deepak.

"Sir, my father lost his business, so he can't support me financially anymore. Now, I can't finance my education," Deepak lied. His father never had a business.

"That's not my problem," the director said in a low, monotone voice as he clicked away.

"Sir, could you possibly find a way so I can pay my tuition? I am a good student," Deepak insisted.

"I don't know whether you're a good student or not, but I know you don't have money." His voice was cold. Deepak's words became tangled up in his throat, and he had to think hard to remember the correct English words.

"Please sir, is there any way you could help me?" Deepak felt a lump rising in his throat and a familiar stinging in his eyes.

"If you can pay the tuition fee, you can study. If not, it is better to go back home to your country. Period!" His voice sounded like the steady hum of a motorbike and his eyes never left the computer screen. "I am not being rude, but that's the truth."

If Bulkio had glanced up at his uninvited guest, he would have seen furrowed brows and an uneasy smile. In his heart, Deepak knew he was probably right. *But this is America, the land of opportunity*, Deepak thought.

Professor Williams also suggested that he go back home. He could not think of the idea of going back home because he knew that was not what he had come to America for.

He was quickly learning that opportunities were more often created in this new country than granted. Success was not haphazard in America; one had to be prepared for the opportunities afforded. Even with preparation, though, unexpected mishaps occur. Was it his fault his father lost his farming business? If Bulkio only realized the struggle his parents had finding the airfare and the few dollars that people had stuffed into his hands as he left home, perhaps he might understand. But would he care? Deepak got the feeling that Bulkio was used to students like him who stood at his door in desperation.

Deepak's hands flailed, making futile gestures. His voice cracked with emotion. "Please sir, don't say that." Deepak trembled with fear at the thought of returning to his home country as a failure in the eyes of himself and the people he had left behind.

"I can do nothing for you. We trusted your bank statement, and we provided you with an I20," he said without lifting his eyes from a computer monitor.

Bulkio was right. Deepak had created a phony bank statement. But it had all been to come to the United States and earn a degree from an American university, to find a job, m a k e enough money to buy a house, care for his parents, and become successful in people's eyes and his own. Wasn't that worth it?

Deepak could see his dreams disintegrating before his eyes. He had mentioned in his application that his father had a poultry farm business and his mother was a teacher, and they earned more than $2,000 per month together. The truth: his father was just a peasant farmer. His mother had never been a teacher. She could read and write, but that was it. Both of them

43

were old, and they worked on the farm for a meager source of income, which had been decimated by a sudden bird flu epidemic. He could still smell the gas they had used to poison the birds and see the large burial mounds where they buried their investments. Yes, he lied to the university, but he was the only hope his parents had as they eked out a shell of existence.

"Did you hear what I said?" Bulkio spoke firmly as his visitor remained silent, rooted to the spot, not even moving an inch from the chair.

Deepak nodded his head and mumbled, "Yes, sir."

The disappointed Deepak slowly got up from the chair prepared to walk out of Bulkio's office, defeat heavy on his shoulders. Before he left, however, an idea popped into his head and he turned around. Bulkio saw him, but pretended not to notice.

"Sir, can you do at least a favor for me?"

Bulkio looked at the file he was reading. "I don't think I can do anything for you."

"I think you can."

"What's that?"

"Sir, just allow me to drop one course from the full load of courses so I don't have to pay the full tuition fee." Deepak thought perhaps the $1500 he currently had could somewhat help him pay the first semester tuition fee if he borrowed a little bit more, if needed, from his closest friend who lived in New Hampshire in the USA.

"I can't do that," he said, glaring up at him with his right hand glued to the mouse.

"Why not, sir?" Deepak tried to sound polite.

"Because you are an international student, you have to have a full load of courses," he said. He started running his stubby fingers over the keyboard. "Right now, I am busy."

"Sir, you know I'm an international student. I have nobody else to help me out if you ignore me." Deepak voice slipped as he began to beg.

"It's not my business. There are many international students who come to me with many problems, sometimes this and sometimes that. You better go home if you can't pay tuition. That's it," he said. His voice raised a couple of octaves, "Do you hear me?"

Deepak's expression shattered. The office splintered before him as his eyes filled with tears. He could not control himself. Streams of hot tears rolled down his cheeks. Deepak just kept repeating, "Sir, please, sir!" He could see a shift in Bulkio's face and saw that the director felt uneasy about the situation.

"Alright, alright! I will let you drop one course," he said, his voice quivering slightly. "But listen, this is your only chance. You can't do it next time, you know!" he warned. Perhaps he just wanted to get him out of his office since others could probably overhear the commotion.

Either way, Deepak felt a wave of relief. "Thank you, sir," he stammered, tears still flowing. With that, he wiped his face with his bare hands and tried to straighten up in his seat. Bulkio's decision helped, but it wouldn't fix everything. He still needed to find a job, and soon.

"Try looking for a job on campus," Bulkio suggested. Deepak nodded.

"Okay, you may go now. I have many things to do," Bulkio added, thumbing through the file in front of him.

Deepak thanked him and left the office before the bulldoggish man could change his mind.

Deepak went to the university library. He was here once but never looked around it seriously. The library was the heart of the university, a red brick building surrounded by Corinthian columns and marble statues of literary figures. Deepak waited in line as some students checked out library books.

"Hello, may I help you, sir?" a librarian with orange, badly permed hair asked.

"Yes, are you hiring now?" Deepak approached her with some hope.

"Not now, sorry, sir!" she said turning her head to the next student who was waiting on line to check out a large pile of books. "Next, how may I help you, ma'am?"

Deepak had thought he could find any on-campus job easily without any big effort, and that is what some of his friends who were in America on a student visa had suggested, but he realized it was easier said than done.

Deepak left the library with the gait of an old man and walked to the university's main computer lab that the director of the International Student Office had hinted at some point. The lab was pristine, mostly white and decked out with new computers. A man approximately in his 30s in a white, button down, collared shirt was sitting at a desk and toying with a computer mouse. After Deepak stood there for a few seconds, the man looked at him and smiled.

"Hi—do you need something?"

"Are you hiring someone for a student assistant position right now?" Deepak said, without any roundabout expression because he realized there was no point of being wordy. He became brief and straight. If they didn't need to hire one, the explanation would be simply useless. If he was in Nepal, or in the context of South Asian countries, he could ask his friends, relatives, or the relative's relative who might have access to find a job, but that technique would be belied in American culture.

"Not yet. I just hired someone two days ago. You can fill this application out, though. If I need someone in the future, I might contact you." He said, giving him a paper application and a pen. *At least he showed some hope*, Deepak said silently.

Deepak filled out the form and gave it back with a smidgen of hope. He then walked toward the bookstore, hoping that he would be granted an inch of luck in his quest to find work on campus.

The bookstore looked welcoming enough, filled with apparel bearing the name and logo of the university and its mascot, a falcon. However, as soon as he got to the front desk, he heard the same tune, "We do not have a position for anyone this semester. You can try again next semester."

As Deepak left, he took out his wallet and counted the bills. He now had around the same amount of money, i.e. $1500. Bulkio had agreed to reduce one course from the full load course that would bring his tuition fee down to the amount of roundabout $2000. He had to pay $300 rent in 15 days. So he thought he needed money at least $2500 within a few weeks to address all the needs. He had no choice; he needed to start looking for a job off campus, if not on campus. At least the university Deepak went to was a lot cheaper than other universities in the US, otherwise the minimum tuition fee per semester could be more than $5000. *I must try to look out for a job,* Deepak realized. He ventured on his mission right away.

He left the university and walked toward a strip mall in the distance. His shirt stuck to his back and large damp spots appeared under his arms before Deepak reached his destination. It took him an hour to reach there. He didn't see any human beings on the road. On the way, the first thing he noticed was a man in a tattered t-shirt and once-blue jeans that were coated with red dirt. He was holding the remains of a piece of a brown cardboard box on which was scrawled: *Need a job. Hungry!*

Have we people like this in America? oh no!, Deepak couldn't believe his eyes. Deepak silently felt his pain. He saw himself walking in a drifter's outfit in the street. Perhaps what he saw relieved him to some extent. Deepak realized sharing pain is mitigating pain.

47

All the shops in the strip mall greeted his work enquiry with uniform negativity. The mall held no hope, so he left. As he walked aimlessly, a Chevron sign appeared in the distance. Deepak decided to try his luck there. His mind was racing. *How can America be the land of opportunity? If I had struggled this much back in Nepal, I would have already found a job or two*, Deepak thought to himself.

"Hello, sir, are you hiring?" Deepak asked, entering the gas station. Its glass door quickly swung shut behind him.

"Hold on a second," a small, thin bald man with a blotchy red face spoke with a long, slow southern drawl. "Let me ask the manager." And the man asked another person in the gas station, perhaps he was the owner or the manager of the store " Hey, Jim, someone here to see yah." Deepak noticed different brands of cigarettes on display by the register and instantly felt the need to smoke. He resisted the urge—he couldn't afford it.

The person came out; the word "Manager" was printed above the pocket of his blue shirt. He was approximately six feet tall and had beard. He gave Deepak a form to fill out, but the application required his social security number.

"Sir, what do I put here if I do not have a social security number yet?" Deepak's voice was hoarse and a bead of sweat ran off the tip of his nose.

"Sorry, we can't accept your application then. You have to have a social security number to work in the U.S. legally. Sorry, man."

Deepak left the gas station dejected. He kept walking on the gravelly pavement. Cars were whizzing by; traffic lights were blinking green, red, and yellow. As Deepak strolled with difficulty on the uneven road with a heavy heart, people walked toward him with placards in their hands. They read "Barak Obama, next president of the US!" Deepak realized these people were marching and campaigning for Barak Obama. News broadcasts were full of unprecedented events as companies and banks lurched and faltered in a recession that stunned the nation.

The sun was scorching. Deepak mopped his face with his fingers and wiped the perspiration on his pants. Tired and hungry, he made it home, went to the kitchen, and drank a cup of water from the tap before lying down on his bed in the living room.

"If you drink water, you won't feel hungry," Deepak remembered what his mother always said. She taught him to ask for water, never food. She thought there was less shame in asking for water. Deepak took money out of his wallet and counted it again. Deepak whispered in exhaustion. He threw the wallet on his bed and looked out the window—the same scene of poplar trees and some squirrels climbing up and down the trees, leaves being colorful along with the fall—a romantic one, indeed.

A soft giggle came from the other bedroom. Vanessa and Lucas were home, Deepak knew. Deepak was quickly starting to hate the lack of privacy in the apartment. In a matter of seconds, giggling was replaced by loud breathing. Deepak kept his eyes glued outside the window, ignoring the now familiar sounds coming from their bedroom. He picked up a yellow diary notepad and began to write:

I am the son of a farmer who tilled the earth from dawn to dusk, drying like a dead fish in the scorching heat, wearing the same used rags as beautiful clothes, no matter where he went, party or palace, bushes or bed. My mom was the cornerstone, who had to collect bundles of branches to build our fire while she had another baby growing like a tender bud in her belly. One meal a day would bring happiness home, while rice would be the food of luxury. I went to school with bare feet and naked body, just wearing underwear, beaten by my teacher every day, who did not understand why I didn't wear proper clothes. When I saw my classmate wearing new things, I asked, mom, why don't have I clothes to wear? Her answer came as tears oozing out from the corners of her eyes. "You have to be a great man," she said.

Deepak thought of the American dream. He splayed on the sofa, staring at the ceiling blankly.

Chapter 7: Friendly Face

I t was another day in the university. Deepak was outside hanging out staring in the distance where students were strolling around while others were sharing kisses with their boyfriends and girlfriends—the same scene Deepak was accustomed to.

The sun was scorching and a few students were sitting under the trees' shade while others were walking toward the cafeteria, some holding hands with their significant others. Deepak saw Lucas walking with a foreign guy near the cafeteria. Before Deepak could call to Lucas, he shouted excitedly at him, causing other students to turn and look in his direction.

"Hey, Deepak, come here!" He walked over to the pair.

"Do you know him?" Lucas gestured to the guy he was with, proud grin on his face. "He's also from Nepal."

Like a puppy meeting another dog on a walk, Deepak's happiness knew no bounds. He looked closely at Lucas's companion. He was of an average Nepali height, about 5 foot 6 inches, with a French-cut beard and a latte-colored complexion. He was dressed in a Polo shirt and black jeans. Deepak's face beamed with pleasure.

"Oh, really?" Excited, Deepak greeted the fellow countryman with a firm handshake. "My name is Deepak."

"I am Ganesh."

"You guys probably have lots to talk about. I gotta go," Lucas said before patting Deepak's back and leaving.

"I am very happy to meet you here in America and, that too, at the university, brother," Deepak said

"There are many Nepali people in America, man.

51

There is nothing to be overjoyed about," he replied in an artificial American accent. He spoke English quickly, though his English sounded somewhat broken.

"How long have you been here, brother?"

"It has been about five years. I am a citizen here." There was a definite pride in his words as he spoke.

"I'm going through a lot, brother! It is good that I found you," Deepak said.

"Why's that?" Ganesh said, standing and playing with the car keys in his hand. Though Deepak attempted to speak in Nepali a couple of times, Ganesh always answered in English.

"I need a job, Ganesh, by hook or by crook. Otherwise, I have to return to the home country, and I cannot continue my education. I did not bring enough money with me. I thought I would find a job easily." Deepak shared his problems with Ganesh, as if he had known him for years. "Since you have been here for a long time, you might know some good places to find a job."

"That's not a big deal," Ganesh said smiling. He seemed to warm a little. "It's not easy to find job in US these days, though."

"I know, brother," Deepak said taking a deep breath.

"You have to be ready to sweep and mop, and that also is not easy to get," Ganesh said. They were still standing and talking; due to the scorching sun, beads of sweat trickled down their faces.

Deepak realized he had to be ready to do whatever he needed if he wanted to fulfill his dreams. *I have to earn a degree, make a lot of money, buy a bungalow back in Nepal, and buy a new car.* Deepak's mind whirled at the thought.

"Did you hear me?" Ganesh seemed slightly annoyed at his silence.

"Oh, yes!" Deepak said quickly trying to cover up his daydreaming.

"You are not going to get any job easily because you have no legal documents to work in the US. You are not a citizen like me." He rubbed the salt into Deepak's wound.

"You're right." Deepak looked into the sky blankly. He saw cumulus clouds hovering over the sky in different shapes and sizes, covering the sun.

"You are hearing me, right?" Ganesh said wiping some sweat that appeared on his forehead.

If I were an American citizen, why should I plead you? Deepak wanted to tell him in Ganesh's face. Instead, he said, "Yes, yes, I was thinking you are the only one here who can help me. I am ready to work, no matter what kind of job it is. I must work.

"Okay, that's not a big deal, bro," Ganesh said.

Overjoyed, Deepak grabbed him in an embrace. "Thank you, brother!"

Ganesh stepped back, visibly shaken. "What the fuck! Don't touch me. Only gays do so. Are you gay?"

Deepak felt jolted by his words and reaction. He stepped back, both mentally and physically. Ganesh's attitude surprised and saddened him. *Why did he speak to me like that?* Deepak thought. The way most people talked and behaved with him had always been very cordial and gentle. Ganesh's attitude made him feel humiliated and dejected.

Was this how American culture changed people? Had Ganesh already forgotten his culture where he was born and raised? Had America taught him to speak that way to one of his own people? Deepak asked these questions to himself and remained silent. He had come to a different land where no one, he felt, would likely understand his anguish at the moment.

"American lifestyle is different," Ganesh said, responding to Deepak's silence. "You are not supposed to embrace each other or walk holding hands with me. A man hugging another man people might think we are gay."

"Oh, really?" Deepak said feeling now like he had broken some cardinal American rule.

Ganesh balked, pointing toward Deepak's shirt, "Shit! See, you are wearing a pink shirt. Only a gay person wears that. Don't wear stuff like that." At that moment, Deepak felt so bad that any initial feelings of camaraderie or friendship with Ganesh vanished. Deepak's face got blushed and ruddy.

"Actually, my sister gave me this shirt in *Bhaitika*, you know, bro," Deepak said looking at his own t-shirt. Deepak became so angry that he thought he needed to remind Ganesh of the culture he was born and raised. "You know *Bhaitika? It is* the second greatest festival of Hindus, also called the festival of lights that is celebrated for five days, once a year. On the fifth day of the festival, sisters pray for their brothers' health and give them gifts..."

"I know, I know, why the fuck are you teaching me this?" Ganesh interrupted him.

"Just making sure!" Deepak said, trying to put a smile on his face in a satirical way.

"Who cares?" Ganesh snorted. "Here nobody cares!"

Oh, god, give me a break, Deepak sighed silently so Ganesh would not hear it. *What kind of stupid person are you to insult me?* Deepak silently cursed him. "What is the possibility of getting a job for me, Ganesh?" Deepak asked, trying to change the subject

"It's not a big deal. Let me try for you, man. I have a few people I can contact. I will call them today."

"Thank you very much, brother," Deepak said putting a smile on his face although he was angry at his attitude. Deepak's mission was to pursue the American dream.

"No problem. Just remember, do for yourself, not for others." Ganesh paced with his car keys in hand. He yielded a frustrated grin before adding. "Don't tell me I am harsh. I am harsh by time, by situation, and by circumstances. You have to fight for every penny here. If you don't have money, nobody is gonna provide for you, pay for you."

Now Deepak guessed why he had sounded so rude.

"I hear you, brother," Deepak said. His voice took on a conciliatory tone.

"If I get a job for you, I will call you. That's not a big deal, but don't be so sure. I have to run now." Ganesh said, adjusting his backpack, giving Deepak his phone number and rushed toward a nearby campus parking lot, with his car keys jingling in his hands. Deepak watched him with an equal measure of hope and distain until the small figure disappeared into the distance and entered the classroom.

Deepak strolled around the campus until it was time to get in the classroom.

Melissa was already in the classroom with her backpack on the side and a few books on the desk. She was thumbing through a poetry book. As soon as she saw Deepak, she made a little space gesticulating for him to sit next to her. They exchanged a few smiles looking into each other's eyes.

"How are you?" she said.

"Fine, and you?"

"Good, I was wondering if you were coming to class, today."

"Wondering if you" pulled a string of Deepak's heart. He remembered Melissa was caring the other day, had offered to drive him home, taught him how Blackboard worked. Today she was in a pink top and mini skirt—her pink color matched with Deepak's shirt that Ganesh had mentioned only gay wore. Not sure of that, Deepak silently thought of the matching chemistry between Melissa and himself.

"The same color, what a coincidence," Melissa whispered to him.

"Indeed," Deepak said with a smile. The professor started lecturing on the significance of symbols and imageries in poetry.

After the class was over, Deepak left the class with Melissa again, and they talked idly, which had become a habit.

Like other times, she offered him a drive home. This time he didn't want to miss that opportunity. He knew it was not Nepal where people seemed to insist as part of showing hospitality and caring, but here in America to keep insisting was to be rude and unkind.

"Sure, thank you," Deepak accepted the offer immediately. Melissa also lived in an apartment complex next to the other side of the road, not far from Deepak's apartment, perhaps a mile away.

They both got in the car. Melissa played music to its lowest volume that it just hummed and echoed inside the car, the music came out very soothing: He realized that he enjoyed spending time with her during those brief moments. He looked at her while she drove—her curvy small frame. They both arrived at Deepak's apartment's parking lot.

"We should hang out sometime," Melissa said, stopping the car and looking into Deepak's face.

"Sure," Deepak said trying to open the door to come out of the car.

"Give me a hug good night," Melissa said welcoming Deepak to hug her. Deepak was not very comfortable with that idea as he was not use to, but thought that was the love and respect coming from Melissa and he cautiously hugged her. Deepak immediately felt her breasts on his chest and the fragrance of shampoo from her hair.

"Good night," Deepak whispered into her ear.

Deepak looked at Melissa once again before he entered the apartment and Melissa was there to wave her hand before she left.

Chapter 8 Sunny Bagel

It was 6 a.m. when Deepak looked at his wristwatch. He was in the living room lying on his bed. He looked out the window and saw the leaves falling on the ground. Some of the trees had started losing the leaves and stood like abandoned lovers waiting. He yawned repeatedly, stitched and turned over on the sofa, rolling over the blanket he had wrapped himself up with. The sofa felt too comfortable to leave.

He thought absently of Melissa. Her face kept appearing in his thoughts, providing just enough motivation to keep him somewhat hopeful. A few squirrels scampered busily around in the poplar leaves outside. At once, he noticed that a few dark hairs had fallen on the bed cover. He fingered his hair, perhaps, he imagined himself balding with hair falling out in clumps. He looked at his hands and the thin skin and measured the bone underneath it. Perhaps he thought he was very skinny. He gathered himself and tried to relax.

He had just borrowed some money from his closest friend in New Hampshire who had been living there on a diversity visa. The money was lent on a condition to pay him back as soon as he would find a job. Thus, he had already paid the tuition fee for the first semester and also had owned a phone from him on his family plan. As soon as he got the phone, he had provided his phone numbers to his friends and family members. Now he needed to find a job as soon as possible to pay the friend's money back, rent, and other expenses.

His cell phone rang, and he saw it was Ganesh's number. A smile lit up his face. Deepak assumed Ganesh found a job. He answered the phone quickly, trying to tame his hope.

"Hello?" "What's up?" Ganesh sounded bossy already. "I got a job for you at a bagel store for you."

"Wow, thank you so much, brother. You made my day!"

"I will be there soon and take you to the place. Be ready." Before Deepak could reply, he had hung up.

If we do not give up, opportunities come by themselves, Deepak thought.

Quickly, Deepak got up from the sofa and went into the bathroom. He shaved off his sparse beard. He pulled a pair of trousers, a black polo shirt and a black jacket out of his luggage. They were slightly wrinkled, but the warmth of his body would soon rid them of this defect. This was going to be his first job in America, so he dressed up nicely. He hummed a song loud to keep up his confidence, inciting the beat of his heart. He looked at himself in the mirror, tucked his shirt in his pants and put the jacket on and again looked at himself all the way from head to heels, posing as if he was in front of a camera.

"Hey, man, you ready?" a voice from outside demanded through the door.

Deepak opened the door to see Ganesh, already impatient. "Hey! Yes, I am almost ready. Come on in, just a second."

"Let's go, let's go. I have no time. I have a meeting. I will wait for you outside. Hurry up." He said looking at the time on his cell phone.

Deepak picked up his backpack and slung it across his shoulders.

"Why are you carrying this, asshole?" he said, pointing toward his backpack. Deepak didn't know what he was talking about. He had never heard the word "asshole" before. He tried to make sense of the word.

"*Asshole?,* What do you mean by Asshole?" Deepak asked him. He looked Ganesh quizzically.

"Your backpack," Ganesh said, giggling.

"Is my backpack an asshole?" Deepak said. He was

59

surprised at his word choice. Ganesh did not answer but just laughed instead and said, "Who cares"? Let's go!"

They climbed down the stairs and got into Ganesh's beat-up Toyota Camry. He played an English song full volume.

After a few minutes' drive, Ganesh parked in front of a bagel store. They got out of the car and walked under huge illuminated letters that read "Sunny Bagel Store." Once inside, Deepak saw a South Asian man of about 5 feet 6 inches filling little round circles of bread with a variety of strange mixtures. He was dressed in khaki shorts with a coordinating khaki-colored shirt. At first glance, he was a blur from head to toe of non-descript beige.

"Hey, Vikas, what's up?" Ganesh spoke to the man in a familiar tone.

"I'm good," The man raised one hand above his head while the other hand was holding a bagel. "How're you?"

"I am fine, thank you. This is my friend Deepak from Nepal. He is the one looking for a job." Ganesh spoke with his phony American accent, removing his sunglasses and placing them on the top of his head as he swaggered from side to side.

The middle-aged man smiled and looked up at Deepak with kind eyes. Vikas left what he was doing and shook hands with them.

"I'm Vikas. Nice to meet you," Vikas said extending his right hand.

"I am Deepak. Nice to meet you, too," Deepak said forcing a smile on his face.

"Have a seat," he said, sounding kind but businesses like, showing them two chairs near him. He looked at Deepak intently. "I own this bagel store. I have been running this store for three years now." Vikas appeared energetic, hardworking and pleasant, often smiling.

60

"I've been living in the US for 10 years as a citizen. I came here from Bangladesh on a diversity visa."

"You were right next to my Nepal," Deepak added.

"Yes, I was," Vikas said.

Deepak instantly scanned Vikas. His clothes were decorated with stains and small holes. Vikas did not look like the owner, rather a trash collector in Nepal.

"The business is very slow. I'm in a situation where I can't just hire anyone, but let's talk a little bit," Vikas added.

The bagel store was relatively large with a high glass counter that separated the customers and the servers. The store had eight tables that attached to the walls. Everything, including the chairs, was painted white and blue. There were already a few customers sitting around the tables and enjoying bagels. Some were reading the *Atlanta-Journal Constitution* while others sipped coffee and talked. The kitchen sizzled and filled the shop with the smell of frying eggs, sausages, and bacon.

"What do you do here?" Vikas asked.

"I go to college."

"Where?"

"Georgia University."

"Speak softly, please," Vikas whispered with a nervous smile. "If somebody finds you working off campus on a student visa, it's gonna be a problem for both of us, you know."

"Oh, I see. Sorry."

"It's okay. How long have you been here?" Vikas quickly changed the subject.

"Just for a month"

"Do you have a car?"

"No."

"Then how do you come to work?

"My friend will drop me off." He glanced at

Ganesh to confirm; Ganesh nodded.

"Is that always possible?"

"I'm going to buy a bicycle next week," Deepak lied as he was not sure whether he would buy or not. First, he needed to make money to do all those things.

"Okay, then," Vikas said. "I can pay only $5 per hour in the beginning. I can increase the wages only after observing your work and how you deal with customers."

Deepak nodded in approval even though he knew the pay was low. Deepak had no other options. This is how they would also take advantage of illegal workers. Deepak thought it was something rather than nothing. At least both of them seemed to be in a win-win situation.

"You have to sweep and mop, too. You should not feel bad," Vikas continued, leaning forward. "Many people who come to the US are not used to sweeping and mopping, so they feel very bad doing this kind of job." Deepak thought Vikas was speaking from his experience.

"Okay," Deepak said slowly, hiding his pain at the thought of sweeping and mopping.

"Have you ever swept?" Vikas seemed to know the answer but asked anyway.

"No. Back in my country, I was an English teacher at a few colleges and wrote books during my academic career," Deepak said immediately. "But I don't mind sweeping and mopping."

"Are you sure?"

"I am sure, sir"

"Then come tomorrow and work for just three hours. Your job will begin then."

"Thank you, sir! See you tomorrow," Deepak said and he and Ganesh left the store. Although Deepak thought the job was more about sweeping and moping, he was excited because he knew he got a job that would pay him. Perhaps, he was mesmerized at the thought that the American dream was coming true.

On the way back home, however, Deepak found his spirits lifting. He started grinning, even singing to himself. Yes, the wages were low, but he had a job. Once more, his dreams shifted from mere illusions to almost tangible possibilities.

"At least I got the job, no matter what kind of job it is," Deepak told Ganesh. "Now I can pay the rent and buy food, although the money I earn from the bagel store might not be enough to pay tuition for every semester. Maybe something fortunate will happen by that time. Anything can happen! I think my luck is changing."

Ganesh did not pay much attention to his words, but rather cranked up the music in his car. In a few minutes, they arrived at Deepak's apartment.

"I am gonna be late, man. I have a meeting," Ganesh repeated while slamming the brakes to stop his car near Deepak's apartment.

"Can't you cancel the meeting today?" Deepak half- heartedly asked, getting out of the car. "And spend some time drinking some coffee and talking with me in my apartment."

"What the fuck are you talking about?" Ganesh's voice raised in exasperation. Deepak just smirked at his crude language and waved his hand at his departing new friend. At least he has found me a job, I don't worry about his attitude, Deepak though silently. *Some people sound rude but are kind by heart.*

Ganesh shut the car door, saying, "See you later."

"Thank you for the job help, brother. Bye," responded Deepak, breathing a sigh of relief before adding, "I will call you."

"I might be busy. You can leave a voice message just in case," Ganesh said, waving Deepak away, rolling down the car window, and screeching off.

At home, Deepak felt elated at the thought of his new job, but then his emotions nosedived as reality hit him in the chest. Deepak sighed. Yes, doors were now starting to crack open, but not as much as he had imagined. His mother used to tell him he was impatient and that he needed to learn to wait. Deepak found waiting difficult. He hated the uncertainty of the American dream.

Contemplative, he sat on the floor of his living space, leaning against the wall. Finally, he pulled himself up and went to the kitchen, looked around and again came back to his previous spot and sat on the floor.

Vanessa and Lucas finally left the bedroom after a time and surfaced into the living room, giggling and chuckling. She was wearing blue shorts and a lacey top that clung and left little to the imagination. On the sofa, Vanessa sat on Lucas's lap. He rocked her gently, and kissed her, purring, "My coy mistress." She laughed, but melted into him. Deepak remembered the poem "To His Coy Mistress" by Andrew Marvell. Deepak always liked the second stanza of the poem, and recited it aloud:

Thy beauty shall no more be found,
Nor, in thy marble vault, shall sound
His echoing song; then worms shall try
That long preserved virginity,
And your quaint honor turns to dust,
And into ashes all his lust...

Vanessa turned her attention to him. "Deepak, How are you?"

Deepak was excited to tell them the news about the job he found at the Bagel store. He wished Melissa was there so he could share the good news with her.

"I got a job, guys," Deepak said.

"Wow, where?" Vanessa said in excitement. "Congratulations, Deepak."

Deepak explained everything and they seemed very happy for him. Deepak remained on the sofa for a while in a jovial mood.

Lucas shifted Vanessa from his lap, went to the refrigerator where he took a carton of ice cream out

64

and started piling some in a bowl.

"Hey, Deepak have some ice cream," Lucas said scooping some in a bowl.

"I am not a fan of cold things, though they are delicious. I avoid them because if I drink something that is too cold, it might create a problem in my throat, like tonsillitis or something. Well, that is what we say in Nepal. But I never know how to refuse others' offers, so I will take it," Deepak stretched his hand out and smiled. "Thank you, Lucas."

"You're welcome." Lucas returned the smile, "You're funny, Deepak, when you say some things. You say so many amusing things." Deepak laughed and his eyes crinkled. Lucas perched on Vanessa's lap like an overgrown lapdog.

Vanessa cuddled Lucas and kissed his lips. Deepak watched them kiss like a crane stares into the azure sky, absently admiring their intimacy. She expressed herself with a few soft Spanish words, pouring her love into him. Deepak could only discern some words she used, such as "amor," meaning love to address her boyfriend.

In Nepal, a husband and wife would not feel comfortable kissing each other while somebody else was present. Here, a boyfriend and girlfriend would openly kiss in public, no matter who was present. *The United States must be the land of excessive personal freedom. Nobody cares about who is doing what,* Deepak mumbled.

Lucas had shifted from Vanessa's lap and pulled her closer. He was wearing shorts that showed his light-colored, hairy legs and blotchy, pink knees. Deepak watched Lucas wrap Vanessa in his arms and glued his chest to her breasts in an embrace that seemed as if they would never part. He poured a flood of kisses on her forehead, brows, eyes, lips, and her cleavage. She responded with a throaty laugh. Deepak felt like the

Statue of Liberty, a blank, silent watcher, with no feelings or ideas of his own. He simply turned away to look out the window, frozen. A cat mewed at their romance.

It wasn't long before they disappeared into their bedroom again. Deepak scooped a small bit of the ice cream, which was starting to melt.

Deepak grabbed his backpack and left for college. *I will tell Melissa about the job,* he continued to think of Melissa. He went to the library for some assignments that needed to be submitted to the professor in class. He had a laptop Vanessa had given to use. The assignment was to submit a poem so he started writing it.

The joy comes from nowhere,
It is within oneself.
Continue to be happy and
To cherish what you do,
To celebrate what you come across,
Joy travels you, and
Opportunities grab you.

He became ready for class. As he came out of the library, he saw Melissa going towards the English building.

"Melissa," he called raising his voice. She turned to him and stopped for him. "I have good news to share with you."

"What's that?" Melissa looked cheerful. She was in a red outfit matching her deep red lipstick.

"I got a job at the Bagel store."

"Wow, congrats!" she said, hugging him "I am happy for you." She had known about how desperately Deepak was looking for a job.

Both entered the classroom. Some of the students had, to some extent, started noticing the closeness of Deepak and Melissa as they always seemed cornered in the room, pretty much in the same location, sitting next to each other. They entered and left the classroom always together. That would be no one's business though. That is how American culture was so it would make no difference at all like in Nepal where people could start backbiting and spreading rumors about someone being in love and intimate before getting married or whatsoever. But Deepak knew, due to the influence of modern culture and media, the society was changing back home too.

All the students submitted the assignment to the professor, discussed the poetry, and listened to the lecture. The class was over.

Melissa and he followed the daily routine—come out of the classroom, go to the parking lot, Melissa driving Deepak home, give a big hug and say "Good night."

"You will be busy now, might not have time to hang out, huh," Melissa said while she stopped at Deepak's parking lot.

"Not really, I work there three/four hours a day and not all days so we can find time," Deepak said.

Melissa tightly hugged him, tighter than previously. Her breasts were pressed harder on Deepak's chest. She hugged and gave a breathing kiss on the side of his neck. Deepak had a fluttering feeling in his chest.

"Good night," both exchanged and waved the hands in loving ways. In Melissa's eyes, Deepak saw the look of love hanging. Melissa left.

Deepak fell asleep crunched against the wall to the sounds of Vanessa and Lucas making love. In his dreams, Melissa patted his head while speaking softly to him. At some point, she turned into Vanessa when she was talking to him.

He awoke from his dream and realized that his neck was aching and one of his legs had fallen asleep. After limping to the bathroom, he made his way back to bed and slept soundly, thinking of the Sunny Bagel where he would go to work the next day.

Chapter 9: Sweat and Tears

Deepak did not have a car, and he had no idea how to navigate the bus route. He decided to leave early and walked to his work place.

As he walked to work for the first time, he did not see a single person walking like him, except for one man in a ragged outfit by a set of traffic lights. He had walked on his own on the streets out there some time ago to look out for a job. That's it.

He saw only cars rushing around him. The streets of Kathmandu came to his mind; there, people gathered in throngs all over the place. Some rode bikes while others rode motorcycles, two or three per motorbike. Many were inside and on the tops of buses; others rode tempos, rickshaws, and taxis. Honking horns deafened; smoke the vehicles emitted would make him cover his mouth and nose. Kathmandu felt suffocated to him.

Here he found the roads clear, clean, and quiet. He enjoyed the humming sound of the cordon of cars in the lane gushing like a river and the blinking lights from red to green to yellow to red.

Deepak found himself walking along American streets as if in a dream. After an hour walk, he finally reached his work place sweaty and exhausted. It was not very difficult to get there as Ganesh had shown the route and it was straight. As he entered the bagel store, Vikas was in the back preparing bagels; his eyes met Deepak's. Some customers were sitting in the chairs and eating bagels. With Vikas, two other workers were taking customers and cleaning.

"You arrived!" Vikas said, that familiar smile lingering on his lips.

"Yes, sir, I have," Deepak responded wiping his

sweat from his forehead. The weather was not that hot but the continuous and fast walking had brought some sweat on his forehead.

"Okay, come inside," he called. "Take off your t-shirt and wear this one." Vikas gave him a t-shirt with a printed tag that read, *Sunny Bagel Store*. Deepak slipped into the restroom and changed into the *Sunny Bagel Store* t-shirt.

"You should also wear shoes, not sandals," he said, pointing to Deepak's gray river sandals. Deepak had brought a pair of leather shoes from Nepal, but didn't have sporty ones that were actually needed for work.

"Okay, I will do so tomorrow." Deepak acknowledged the rebuke without another word.

"See, your hair is long. You have to cut your hair or wear a cap to cover it," Vikas said, pulling a lock of Deepak's long hair.

It was true, Deepak had not gotten a chance to get his haircut before he got to the U.S., and it was very expensive. He could have gotten his hair cut a dozen times in Nepal with the money it cost to get his hair cut once in the US.

"It is very expensive here," Deepak said.

Vikas laughed. "You should cut your hair, anyway," he said, putting the bagels he had filled in a bag.

"Yes, Vikas," Deepak answered. In the meantime, he thought wearing a cap would be perhaps cheaper.

"Okay, now, you start sweeping," Vikas ordered him, handing him a broom and pointing it to the place where Deepak was supposed to sweep. Deepak looked around the place; it was wide from the kitchen, the store, all the way to the front where customers were eating bagels.

Deepak felt humiliated although he was mentally prepared to sweep the floors in front of customers. With the broom in his hand, he remembered his work environment back in Nepal: a big classroom where students would listen to his lectures. Deepak imagined himself surrounded by students and took a poem by Robert Burns, "My Love is Like a Red, Red Rose." He read and interpreted the poem to the students. Taking chalk, Deepak wrote lines down on the blackboard and dusted off the dirt from his coat, pants, and tie. But then Deepak opened his eyes and saw the broom in his hand. He couldn't move his feet readily while sweeping; his hands and legs felt heavy. His eyes began to burn, he felt nauseous, and, out of nowhere, a headache appeared.

He began to shake inwardly. He had only two options: either sweep the floor or go back to Nepal. *If you want to achieve the American dream, begin your career by sweeping the floor,* Deepak talked to himself silently. He gathered confidence with an inner voice in his heart, repeating the mantra with every brushstroke. *Sweep, Deepak, sweep. The American dream is not that far.* Deepak inhaled sharply and exhaled with a long breath and continued sweeping until he had finished.

"You need to practice to sweep very quickly and carefully," Vikas told him from the kitchen while frying eggs in a large frying pan. Customers in the store wouldn't hear or would not care about the conversation they had.

"I am trying," Deepak said. He didn't want to show Vikas his humiliation, although he felt that Vikas could read his face.

Vikas called two other workers and introduced them to the new recruit.

"He is Deepak from Nepal," he said. "And this is Margareta and Daniel, from Mexico."

"Nice to meet you," Deepak said. Margareta and Daniel looked at each other and chuckled. Perhaps they found the name *Deepak* weird or bizarre.

"Nice to meet you," they said in one voice, evenly.

"You can shadow them. Mimic what they say and do," Vikas said and returned to them and said again

"Train him."

"Yes, sir," Deepak and others said, bowing down his head a bit with respect.

"Follow me," Daniel said immediately.

Deepak did as he was told. Daniel was short with a round face and kind brown eyes. He taught Deepak how to make bagels and serve the customers, how to collect trash, and how to wash dishes. Daniel was 17 and became his mentor at the bagel store for a few days. Deepak knew Daniel probably did not know or understand the landslide of feelings he was experiencing since, as Daniel told him, the work he did in Mexico was much the same.

Deepak couldn't accept the idea of a younger and less educated person teaching an older and more educated one. He was never exposed to the culture that ever taught work is work and no work is smaller or bigger. Nor did he know that a mentor could be anyone depending upon the experience and knowledge of the work. He was biased with the idea that academic qualification is all in all and that should define the superiority and inferiority of people. The Nepali education system had failed to introduce him to the idea of what education was really for. That is why it became so hard for him to accept the truth he faced in the bagel store.

Take the order of a customer, toast the bagel if they want, cut it in half, fry an egg, or bacon, or sausage, or whatever the customers want. Put cheese, butter, or cream cheese on the bagel. Pack it, and give it to them. Then go to the register and ring it up. Clean everything if there are no customers, keep track of everything, and throw out the trash, sweep, and mop.

Deepak worked like a machine, according to the orders and instructions of his co-workers.

I hate this. I hate doing this job, but I am going to do it and be damn good at it, Deepak fumed inwardly.

"Go ahead and take the customer," Daniel

71

ordered him while Deepak was washing dishes. He dried his hands on his shirt and quickly approached the customer. "Hello sir, how can I help you?"

"Yes, give me an Everything bagel," the customer ordered. Deepak didn't understand him, so he remained silent. Daniel came to his aid and went to the box of bagels, picking one up and showing it to him. "This is the Everything bagel," he informed Deepak after the customer left. Deepak didn't even realize that "Everything" was the name of the bagel. He thought the customer was asking for all kinds of bagels.

"I had never heard of bagels in my life before I came to the U.S.," Deepak explained to Daniel. Daniel just laughed. Deepak tried to wrap his mind around all the different kinds of bagels: everything, garlic, onion, sundried tomato, sesame, cinnamon raisin, plain, egg, herb, and many more.

In the beginning, he could not even understand the native accent and colloquial words clearly, and he had to ask customers two or three times for their order. One customer complained, "Why'd you hire someone who doesn't understand English?"

"You go and collect the garbage," Daniel ordered him. "I'll take the customer. And I will show you where to throw"

Deepak collected garbage and both of them went to throw out the trash. The dumpster behind the bagel store was so rank that Deepak could hardly tolerate the noxious odor. He covered his nose and mouth to block the smell, but it could not be masked easily. He took out his handkerchief from his wallet, and remembered his sister, who had given it to him at *Tihar*.

"Throw there," Daniel's voice boomed at him. A little authority went a long way and he acted like Deepak's boss. Deepak again felt humiliated to have a younger and less-qualified person lord over him. Once again, his dreams seemed hollow and he wondered if it was worth it. Deep inside, he realized that more than anything, it was his pride that hurt.

Mopping and sweeping were not physically hard tasks, but mentally they seared into his brain and made him feel like dirt. Misery lined his face with every sweep of a broom or mop. He felt like his heart was breaking into a million pieces, never to be collected again. He wanted to shout and let all the workers at the bagel store know that he could not work anymore, that he would rather go back to Nepal and start teaching at a college. But he thought of the American dream again and realized that was not a good idea. He fought his own thoughts.

He imagined himself talking to his mother to book a plane ticket to return home. Subconsciously, as the son of a Brahman, one of the elites in the caste system, to handle trash was to have sunk to the level of the lowest group in society. He claimed he did not believe in the caste system, but every time, when he reached the Dumpster, he felt humiliated.

This is just the work. I have come here to get my future. I have many things to do in my life. The work is not superior or inferior in itself, but it is my feeling that makes it so. New experiences in my life will make me a mature person. These experiences should be the source of my progress, he talked to himself silently, worked hard to control his emotions, and remained strong.

Deepak wrestled between the desire to stay in America and his hatred of the menial job. *I cannot kill my pride and feelings. I cannot live this life. I am dead emotionally,* he mumbled. Humiliation mixed with disgust and feelings of hopelessness consumed him. He could do nothing, except work. Money made the world go around. Without it, he was lost. Fees, rent, food all cost money and this was just one side of the coin.

He thought each and every person in America was after money. Even a penny mattered here. It was just the opposite of what he had thought before coming to the US. Capitalism had swallowed the country. Nobody would even pee if you didn't pay for it. He hated America, rather he preferred a peaceful life back home. He thought of Karl Marx and his ideas on capitalism. He mulled over his teaching on how capitalism alienated people while replacing humanity with money.

But the practical life hit him very hard. He needed to send money back to his parents. They were expecting it and needed it. His mother's diabetes was costing money that his parents did not have.

While Deepak was contemplating and working, Vikas came to him and said, "Deepak, I also have a sandwich store called Succulent Sandwiches in the Mall. You can work there, too. So be very quick to learn things in here if you need more hours."

Actually, that was good news for him because he desperately needed more hours. He was recognizing the importance of money.

"Alright, I'll do my best." Nodding his head in approval, with excitement and anxiousness- excitement because he was going to work more hours and make more money, anxious because he wasn't sure if he could take any more jobs like this.

After the first day's work in the bagel store was over, he walked back home. Everything was still strange and new to him: the people, places, roads, and vehicles. He walked taking small steps; his shoulders drooped as much as his eyes did. The winter was on its way but the sun was still scorching; exhaustion engulfed him.

By the time he got home, his feet were tired, but he had a class to take in the evening. His feet refused to move anymore once inside the apartment, but with the excitement of meeting Melissa in class later, all of his pain disappeared.

After a bit of rest and a nap on the sofa, Deepak ate something from the refrigerator and headed to college.

He entered the library, did some assignments sitting in front of a library computer. There were rows and columns of computers and students were using their fingers on the keyboards deftly. An insistent and persistent noise from the keyboard was echoing. No sooner did Deepak look at Mellissa, than she saw him and said, gesturing to come closer to her "Hi."

'You are here too," Deepak said walking to her and sitting in a chair next to her. "I also have to print the assignment." He turned on the computer while speaking with Melissa.

"Let me also finish it," Melissa said with her eyes on the computer screen and her fingers on the keyboard. Deepak looked at her moving fingers on the keyboard— long and the nail painted red. They occasionally exchanged glances and smiles as they worked on the computer.

It was 6 pm, they headed to class.

With the class over, the routine was the same—walk to the parking lot, drive together to Deepak's apartment, hug each other, exchange a few smiles, and say "goodbye." It had become customary.

As he entered the apartment, he flopped on his sofa and thoughts of Melissa entered and soothed him. He never thought he could go for anyone but a Nepali girl. Having an American girlfriend was not on his radar before. His life was mapped out like those of his friends before him. They had returned to Nepal where their fathers and close family members had suggested a couple of eligible women. They looked at the women's pictures and, if they were pretty, then they would agree to meet them. Once they met a girl, they would say "yes" or "no," depending on a five-minute conversation that the woman and man would have on their own. If yes, they would be fed candies, and the next day, the marriage shopping would be completed. The wedding would take place the day after, or on a date the parents fixed with the bride and groom's consent.

The complicated nature of meeting someone, falling in love, and winning over someone's heart was not something Deepak expected or thought he wanted. Deepak was learning, as many had done before, that love came in unannounced.

He slept soundly for the first time in a long time, comforted by these thoughts.

Chapter 10: Succulent Sandwiches

Deepak woke up still sore from his previous day's work, but in a better mood. At least he was on the right track now. He pulled up the window blinds to look outside and watch the dawn break; he saw trees and bushes, a faded version of their verdant color. Dried, multi-colored leaves were festooned on the ground and on the tops of bushes. They obscured the white parking lines in the courtyard. It was the month of November already.

He had a number of assignments to turn in for his evening feature writing class. If he missed the deadlines, his instructor would lower his grade. He also had to get to the bagel store on time for work; otherwise, he might be fired. If he were fired, the repercussions would be dire. The word "tuition" floated before his eyes. He had to be ready for his next semester. Deepak talked himself through his situation.

Since all of his classes were in the evening, he could work during the day. This meant working a six-hour shift and then going to class even if he was exhausted. He could do his assignments at midnight and, if he was lucky, catch four hours of sleep a day. Deepak felt optimistic. He reached for a book from the table close to his bed and read a few pages before jotting down notes on the laptop for his assignment.

His classes weren't getting much easier. Surrounded by white and black students, Deepak speculated he was the only international student in the class. Every time Deepak spoke to the class, all the students stifled a laugh at his pronunciation. Melissa was the only one to jump to his defense, glaring at the jeering students.

77

"That sounds good," Mellissa said, looking at him and around the peers in the class.

Deepak reached out to the laptop Vanessa had given next to him and opened it that showed the time 7:15 a.m. *Shit, it is late! I must get to work on time*, he said aloud.

Deepak leaped up from the bed to the kitchen and grabbed a slice of bread for breakfast before he left for work. He spread peanut butter over the bread and downed a sip of coffee that Lucas or Vanessa had left. He tugged on his uniform, pulling it over his head before rushing through morning traffic on foot.

As soon as he got there, Vikas told him that he would take him to his Succulent Sandwiches store in the mall.

"Let's get in the car," Vikas sniffed. His teeth showed in a half grin as he spoke.

Vikas drove them over in his silver Toyota Camry and parked outside the mall's main entrance. The mall was beautiful with its carpeted display aisles and chic red leather sofas scattered with precision here and there. He was spellbound by the variety of different stores, each with their own beautiful lights and decorative designs. Victoria's Secret, Bath and Body Works, Abercrombie and Fitch, Chick-fil-A, Coach, Godiva Chocolatier, and Vitamin World beckoned to Deepak.

Their strange names conjured up a million and one unfulfilled dreams. Ladies with skimpy dresses and long legs stood near the doors of the stores and greeted customers with plastic smiles as they passed by. Silver escalators carried a flow of people through the mall. In the distance, Deepak saw golden letters that read: Succulent Sandwiches. It was situated between Golden Mandarin and American Cajun fast food stores. As they got closer, Deepak could see that it was less of a store and more of a counter with a cash register and a food display.

An older woman, perhaps in her late 40s, was

working at the cash register.

Vikas introduced him to her. "Her name is Rita. She is also from Nepal."

"Oh, really?" Deepak said surprised and then turned to the woman. "Didi Namaskar," Deepak said, shyly, greeting her in their familiar tongue. He was happy to find a person from Nepal here. He felt a little more at home already.

Vikas left Deepak, saying breathlessly, "You will work with Rita," and, turning to Rita, told her, "Please train him. I have to go to the other store. Call me if you need anything." With that, Vikas left.

Rita looked tired but anxious to begin.

"Bhai, when did you come to the USA?" Rita said, wiping the white counter to remove the breadcrumbs and lettuce.

By calling each other *Bhai* and *Didi*, they established a brother-sister type relationship.

"Just a few months now, *Didi.*"

"Do you like it?"

"Yes," he said, "but I am already tired with the work they have us doing."

"This is America, *Bhai.* They don't be tired," she scowled.

"Sweeping, moping, washing is really tiring, *didi*," Deepak added.

"*Bhai,* I started sweeping and mopping when I came to America, which I had never done before in my life. It is not only you. There are some people who were government officials back in Nepal and who now work at restaurants here in the U.S." Her voice rose and her head nodded from side to side as she spoke.

"Really?" Deepak said, just looking at her talking while working.

"*Bhai,* my husband was a government official. Now he works at a restaurant. I have been living in America for four years with my family: my husband and our daughter. I have a good economic status back in Nepal; I have a five-story home and a car." In Nepal, owning a car was a sign of wealth, where, in the U.S., even poor families could own a car.

A customer appeared and Rita motioned with her hands, "*Bhai*, hold on." She turned to the customer and switched back to English. "Hello, sir, how may I help you?"

"Just looking," the customer said and left. She again returned to Deepak swearing silently in Nepali at the customer. "*Sala bhate*, asshole, why do you look if you don't want to eat?" she said and turned to Depaak. "*Bhai*, in Nepal, I hired a worker to sweep and mop my house. Here, I am sweeping and mopping."

Deepak only nodded, listening closely to her words. Rita was a short woman, maybe a couple inches over five feet, with a flat face that masked her energy and perseverance. Despite the hard work, she seemed content with what she was doing. When Deepak asked her about it, she replied, "*Bhai*, I am happy here because the money I make working at the Succulent Sandwiches is five times more than what I was earning as a teacher back in Nepal."

Deepak again nodded. He'd come from similar circumstances.

"I can earn a month's worth salary back in Nepal within a day here in the U.S.," she continued, a smile drawing over her face. The rag in her hand swung back and forth, cleaning the counter as she spoke. They were once again interrupted by the voice of a customer.

"Hello, can I help you, sir?" she asked, turning back to the customer. She took his order and began to work on it. Deepak watched her hands move, silently taking notes. Cutting a loaf of wheat bread in half, she said to Deepak, "I have been working at Succulent Sandwiches f o r three years. I work 70 hours a week making sandwiches, sweeping, and mopping."

Deepak noticed the customer looked irritated by their conversation, but Rita didn't seem to pay him any attention.

After she made the customer's sandwich, she rang the sandwich up, and said to the customer, "Thank you, have a good day!" The customer left without so much as another word, and she turned back to Deepak. "I do hard work because I have to. *Bhai*, my child is studying here. I have to think about her future. I cannot support her without working, no matter how wealthy I am in my country."

"I know," Deepak said, then admitted, "I don't know the first thing about making a sandwich. *Didi*, will you teach me?"

"Don't worry, *Bhai*," she said. "But when I teach you, you might want to keep me under your feet when you are trained"

Deepak couldn't understand what she meant by that, but he held his tongue. "Is she warning me not to act superior over her after she trains me?" Deepak wondered.

He tried not to think too hard about it—instead, he focused his attention on the customers walking around through the mall.

"*Bhai*, take off your Sunny Bagel shirt and put on this one," Rita said, handing him a Succulent Sandwiches shirt. Deepak did as he was told, switching into the Succulent Sandwiches uniform, which was a red polo shirt with the words Succulent Sandwiches in large yellow letters across the front. She taught Deepak how to make sandwiches and familiarized him with the different toppings he would be using.

She even taught him how to sweep and mop, which the people at Sunny Bagel hadn't bothered to show him. Deepak seemed to be learning more quickly than in Sunny Bagel. *Learning depends on the mentor*, Deepak then thought.

Rita had a sharp voice when she spoke as she swept the broom across the floor, demonstrating for him. "Everyone who comes to America does the same kind of work that I am doing, no matter what they used to do or how wealthy they were in Nepal," she repeated. "*Bhai,* you have to try to learn how do to things as quickly as you can."

Rita took a customer's order and told Deepak to fill it. He tried to make the sandwich as she'd taught him, but he could not discern some of the ingredients.

"*Didi,* what is mustard?" Deepak asked.

"You cannot read," she raised her voice as if she was scolding. Her voice rose in a demeaning manner, as she pointed to the bottle of mustard that had the word "*mustard*" printed on front.

Deepak felt ashamed when she chastised him. She could read it in his face, and added, a little softer, "My blood pressure is high. I might lose my temper easily." Deepak couldn't figure out whether it was an apology or a warning.

"*Bhai,* I caught blood pressure," she continued. "My blood pressure has been high since my mind was haunted with the thought of my home in Nepal collapsing after I heard the news about an earthquake uprooting many buildings in India."

Deepak tried to pay attention, but she droned on and on. He quickly grew tired of listening to her. The store was slow so she spent every free second chatting. Deepak looked for something to busy himself with rather than listen to her and found a broom. He started sweeping in the furthest corner.

"If you do not know how to sweep and mop, nobody is going to give you a job," she said, watching him as if he was auditioning. "Sweeping and mopping is the common thing for many Nepali people in the U.S."

"Oh, really" Deepak flashed a pretentious smile.

"You didn't even know that," she retorted. "At

least Vikas is kind. The first owner I worked with, he was horrible. Did I tell you about him?"

"You did," Deepak said. Rita had already mentioned him about that.

"That's how it works in America, *Bhai,*" she said grabbing the broom from Deepak. "Give me this. You learned nothing. I will show you how to sweep." With that, she started sweeping again. Deepak had thought he knew it more quickly but realized he was still slow.

"My father used to say, if you don't study and get a good degree, you will have to sweep and mop," Deepak said with a light, bitter laugh. "Now that I have my college degree in Nepal, I still have to sweep and mop."

"Your degree in Nepal is not going to help you here, *Bhai,*" She laughed caustically. "I also have a degree in Nepali literature. What can I do?"

You can do nothing with your degree in Nepali literature in an English speaking country, Deepak wanted to say. *There is no point of bragging about Nepali degree in an English speaking country. Even though my major is in English, I ended up sweeping and mopping all the same.* But Deepak didn't say anything. *This lady is a dual nature,* Deepak mumbled and fumbled.

One moment, Rita seemed very kind and generous, and at other times, she seemed very mean and rude in the way she talked to Deepak.

She spent the rest of the day teaching Deepak the different sandwiches and talking his ear off. After a few hours' work, she said, "I think, you're almost done for today. Do you want me to make a sandwich for you?"

"Sure, *Didi!*" Deepak said, gladly accepting her offer. She made a chicken sandwich and handed it over to him. He thanked her, nodded his head politely, and added, "See you tomorrow!"

Since it was his first day, he had gotten out early. He walked back to the apartment, went to college

83

for class, and returned home at 7 p.m., exhausted. Melissa brought him home- the same schedule. As soon as he came back to the apartment, he dosed on the sofa, leaning against for a few minutes.

He woke up thirsty and hungry and tried to eat the wrapped sandwich Rita had made for him that afternoon. He had never eaten a sandwich before and he found he did not like the taste or texture of it. Instead, he walked to the refrigerator and hunted for food. He settled on leftover rice and scrambled eggs and drank a glass of water.

Before he went to sleep, he opened the laptop and turned on a Nepali online radio station, hoping the songs would put him to sleep. Songs rang out with lyrics praising the gods and goddesses who had victory over evil, which was celebrated during Nepal's biggest and longest festival of the year. As he listened, he realized that today was *Dashain* in Nepal. He wondered why Rita had not mentioned it and if she had forgotten about it.

Alone in the apartment, Deepak could see it was dark outside. The trees looked like ghosts with many hands, leaves hanging like hair. He knew the days were becoming gradually shorter and nights were becoming longer as they welcomed Christmas across the U.S. It was cold out there.

Dashain was probably in full swing back in Nepal. Missing this year's Dashain weighed heavily on him, as the online radio blared the program host's voice that talked about Dashain:

"*Dashain*, the greatest festival of Hindus, is celebrated in every house in Nepal. Since today is the first of 5 days of *Dashain*, young and old, children and women, all of them have smiles on their faces. Everyone looks colorful in new dresses and raiment. Juniors are receiving blessings with tika from the hands of their parents, and seniors are busy putting tika on the foreheads of juniors. During the entire15 days of

Dashain, people visit their families and relatives and exchange their joys and happiness, forgetting every painful event in their lives.

They enjoy varieties of delicious foods, regardless of age and sex. No matter how rich or poor they are, they celebrate *Dashain* with great enthusiasm. In *Dashain*, the relatives of their family also return from abroad to receive tika from the hands of seniors...."

He could not listen to the news anymore because it reminded him of many things he missed back home. He pictured his parents putting "tika," a mixture of rice, yogurt and vermillion for coloring, on his forehead, blessing him so that he would receive happiness, prosperity, and a good reputation. His parents would chant the *Dashain* blessing mantra, "*Aayundra Nasute srinta Dasarathe, Satru Chhayngra Gave...*" that indicates the victory over evils. His sisters and Deepak would line up on the carpeted floor by a plate full of *achayata*, flowers, and money bills. He would touch his parents' feet with his head to pay respect.

Overwhelmed, Deepak lay on the sofa with his face down and the pillow above and moaned silently, *I missed it, I missed it.*

Outside, it was getting darker and slowly the trees were swallowed by the darkness, removing any hint of their shadows. Streaks of rough lightening haphazardly illuminated nature and showed the hovering clouds. Intermittently, Deepak saw and heard squirrels as they chattered loudly in the trees, as if complaining about their lot on a wet, dreary night. Likewise, Deepak grumbled to himself. *Dashain should have been delayed until next year. Why does it come every year?*

Soon, Deepak felt very hot and sweaty. He cracked open the window to let in some air, but it wasn't enough, so he left the apartment and walked over to the courtyard. The temperature was 65 degree Fahrenheit.

Once outside, Deepak decided to walk over to the

gas station to buy cigarettes. As he walked down the street, cars rushed by him. Two lovers stood intertwined on the corner of the sidewalk, hiding their heads in their embrace, blocking his way. In the dark, they looked like twisted shadows. He quickly stepped around them; they didn't seem to notice him.

Deepak reached the gas station and bought a pack of Newport cigarettes. Once outside, he lit one. It wasn't as good as a Nepali cigarette, but it would do. As he started walking home, he felt a dizziness sweep over him; the sidewalk revolved around him. He sat down on the ground outside the gas station until his dizziness was gone. With that, he got up and began to walk back to his apartment, again stepping around the entwined couple. The sounds of their kissing rubbed him the wrong way. He heard enough of that at home, and every time, he felt a pang of loneliness. *Keep me away from this sound,* Deepak murmured and rushed home.

It was midnight by the time he got home. The online Nepali radio had shifted to Nepali classic music, welcoming the enchantment of the *Dashain* festival across the country. On the computer, Deepak browsed Nepali sites. They were filled with pictures of goddesses and devils, signifying the victory of good over evil, and pictures of people putting *tikas* on the foreheads of children. The music and photographs brought up a multitude of feelings that engulfed him.

He left the apartment to light another cigarette. It'd been so long since he'd had them, now he was craving one. However, he wasn't alone, and a man approached him on his porch.

"What's up, man?" the stranger asked generously. "Can I have a cigarette?" The stink of alcohol came from the stranger's mouth. The man looked in his twenties, with a dark complexion and curly dreadlocks that touched his shoulders. In one hand, he held up his pants, which were falling around his hips, and the other hand

86

was busy playing music on his cell phone, which he clutched to his ear.

"Sure, sir," Deepak said. He tried to sound confident and polite. Deepak took a cigarette and gave it to the stranger.

"Thanks, man," the stranger said and left.

Deepak finished smoking quickly and returned to the apartment. There, he closed the door and locked himself in.

It was 2 a.m., as he lay on his bed, but he could not fall asleep. Instead, he kept staring at the wall.

In his memory, his parents were laughing, having a good time and making merry. His mother and father and other relatives were around him, eating a mountain of delicious foods. There were apples, bananas, blueberries, *Makhhan*, yogurt, *Chiura*, beaten rice, oranges, goat meat and many other dishes around the table. The scent was heavenly. Spicy and sweet aromas tickled his nose. He talked to his family and laughed until he felt like bursting with happiness. Deepak watched his relatives putting *tika* on his sister's forehead. Outside, the sound of kids laughing as they played on the swings and flew their kites in the courtyard added to the festive atmosphere.

A sense of nothingness invaded his senses. He felt his eyes once again become teary. He wiped them with his hands. The more Deepak wiped, the more useless his actions became. *Unabated streams of tears rolled down his cheeks. I am missing everything, Mom,* Deepak cried inwardly. *I missed the mutton and sell roti you make. I missed the akchhyata you put on my forehead. I miss you, Mom.*

Suddenly, his phone rang. Deepak grabbed the phone and tried to sound normal when he said, "Hello?"

"Hello!" A wave of emotion pooled into his heart at his father's voice on the other end.

87

"Yes, *Buwa*, how are you? Deepak said. "How is *Dashain* going?"

"We miss you a lot. We cannot even celebrate *Dashain*. Your mother is very sad."

"Would you please give her the phone?"

Deepak's mother started crying on the phone, saying, "I would like to see you. Come home."

"No Mom, it's not possible to come now. I have to wait a year and a half to graduate."

"Without you, we have no taste for Dashain," she said in a staccato voice. "Without you, Dashain is like Dasha," meaning a blessing was like a curse.

"Don't say that, Mommy! There are many mothers who lost their sons in the long, 10-year war between the Maoists and security forces. Their sons never came back home. But I am here, struggling for an American dream. I am going to be there after I graduate."

Deepak heard her sobbing as he spoke. He could not listen to her cry anymore since it weighed heavy on his heart, so he said, "I have to go, Mommy. I love you. Bye."

He hung up the phone, his loneliness persistent. "You will never know how much I am crying and missing everyone and everything, Mom, but that is a part of the sacrifice that we have to make to change our lives," Deepak wrote in his diary near his pillow. Deepak knew in his heart that struggling was inevitable if he wanted to change his life. He buried his head in his pillow and, eventually, his exhausted soul and body fell asleep.

Over the next couple of weeks, Deepak strangled his negative thoughts and reminded himself of his need for money. He continued working, making bagels, sweeping the floor, taking the customer's orders, and washing the dishes with a growing sense of pride. Soon, he was working just as diligently as some of the other employees who had been there longer.

Chapter 11: Surviving

When Deepak opened the fridge to make breakfast the next morning, there was nothing in it except for some stinking cheese and bread tinged with a furry grey coating. He had to go to the grocery store. He looked around for a pen and found a piece of lined paper in his backpack to make a list of things he wanted to buy. "Bread, peanut butter, rice, fruit, vegetables, juice..." As the list grew, he knew he would need a ride so he knocked on Vanessa's door.

"Hey, Vanessa," he called out.

Lucas answered the door instead. "She is not here, man. She'll be back in an hour. She went out for a morning run. Why do you need her?"

"Actually, I have to go to the grocery store because I have nothing left to cook. I thought that Vanessa might take me to the store."

"Sure. Just wait until she gets back. I'll go with you."

Sure enough, Vanessa came back an hour later and agreed to drive them. The three of them clambered in the car and left for the store. As usual, Vanessa drove and Lucas made himself comfortable in the front passenger seat, fastening his seatbelt.

"Have you ever fallen in love, Deepak?" Vanessa asked bluntly when she noticed Deepak's eyes lingering on the couple's entwined fingers.

Her question made Deepak nostalgic. "No, actually," he said, taking a long breath. "I was in a relationship with a young girl once. Her name was Anita." Deepak become slightly shy recounting the story. "But it was a kind of passionate love that came and went like the wind. I was a teenager then. My mom would call it a *kukhure bains*, a chicken youth," and Deepak laughed.

Lucas and Vanessa laughed, saying, "You're funny!" Lucas popped in his ear buds and listened to music while Vanessa focused on driving. Anita's image stirred in Deepak's mind.

Anita was 16 at the time with a perfect white smile, long hair, beautiful chestnut brown eyes, and luscious lips. She stood taller than Deepak, and her big breasts were as spellbinding as the breasts of a statue angel. It was June when they got together, the month of the rainy season in Nepal. The farmers were busy planting rice on their farms as the two took regular strolls along on the terrace. The view around was panoramic, mountains in all four directions. Kanchenjunga and Mount Everest could be seen at a distance, watching over them. Anita and Deepak walked together, shoulder to shoulder. They then sat on the hammock on the farm when the sun hid its face in the horizon and kissed each other playfully. She embraced Deepak, and he felt like a little baby in her arms with his head in between her breasts.

Vanessa braked heavily at the parking garage. The jolt halted Deepak's daydreaming.

Wal-Mart announced its existence in large yellow letters above the entrance gate. Deepak followed Vanessa with one of the shopping carts that were left outside. They did not have shopping carts in Nepal, and he had a little trouble navigating it. As he entered the Wal-Mart, the cool temperature inside brought a chilling sensation from the tip of his toes to the top of his head. He hugged himself.

"Are you cold, Deepak?" Vanessa asked. "Yes, it's freezing in here"

At a glance, Wal-Mart looked like a showcase decorated with lots of brightly packaged groceries for customers to view. Multicolored goods were arranged under various categories and stacked along the aisles. The smell of hot bread permeated the air. Deepak remembered reading somewhere that this was a trick that stores used to entice their customers. He also recalled reading that the edges of the supermarket were where one should shop, as they usually had bargains.

Deepak's eyes roamed, some workers were replenishing goods on the shelves, and others were ringing up customers' purchases at the registers. The lines were long, and people shuffled impatiently waiting to pay. The self-service registers had only two or three people checking out their merchandise. The aggravation of the overly sensitive, often malfunctioning self- service machine was too much to take at times, so people preferred to wait for an actual cashier, no matter how long the line.

Deepak bought $40 worth of groceries, including a cap for $10 to wear at Succulent Sandwiches and he spent $20 on the cheapest pair of shoes he could find for work.

Forty dollars was worth a month's rent in Nepal. "This is too much money," Deepak fussed in a panic as he stood by the cash register. He had collected some money from his work the other day. He paid the money and returned home, quickly getting to work chopping cauliflower and potatoes into tiny pieces to make curry. He poured rice into the bottom of a pressure cooker he had brought from Nepal, measuring the depth of the rice with his thumb so that he knew how much water to add.

The pressure cooker whistled, whooshed, and spluttered. The noise brought Lucas peeking into the kitchen. "Hey, man, what the heck is going on in here?" It was the first time Deepak had used the pressure cooker in the apartment, and it was clear by Lucas' expression that he had never seen one before. Deepak guessed he was a child of the microwave age.

After Deepak explained how the pressure cooker

worked, Lucas laughed and said, "Funny!"

Deepak turned on the laptop and listened to BBC Nepali news while cooking on the stove. The rice and curry took around 20 minutes to cook. He piled rice high on a plate, cut a cucumber up in chunks and placed them in a small bowl. He spooned golden curry into another bowl and gorged himself on all three.

Feeling full to capacity, Deepak glanced at his wrist watch. It was noon, almost time to go to the bagel store. *I have to fight for each penny,* he murmured. He mentally counted the money he made working four hours the previous day. He did the math and figured that, at $5 an hour, he probably made a total of $20. He calculated how many hours a week he had to work to pay his tuition for a semester, plus rent, and other day-to-day bills. He figured he had to earn at least $1,500 per month. That was not going to be easy. Deepak sighed heavily, suddenly feeling tired, tired of everything.

Vanessa stepped in behind him looking for something in the closet.

"What time do you have to work, Deepak?" Vanessa asked, taking a pair of fairly new tennis shoes out of the closet.

"Right now, but I don't know how I will get there because it is already too late."

"I will drop you off if you want," Vanessa said.

"Thank you so much, Vanessa," Deepak said putting a warm smile on his face. "I am very thankful to you." At least he was lucky to have roommates that looked out for him.

"No problem," Vanessa said, flashing a smile.

In the car, they took their usual places: Lucas in the passenger seat, Vanessa driving, and Deepak admiring from behind. The windows were rolled down and Vanessa's long curly hair played a game of hide-and-seek with the wind. Every now and then, she used a hand to swish a lock that had blown across her face. Deepak found himself admiring her—her hair, her face, her shoulders, and her breasts. Whoever and whatever she might be, she seemed to care about Deepak, and it made him happy.

She dropped him off at the bagel store, where Vikas was filling bagels and left saying, "Bye, Deepak. See you tonight. Don't work hard."

"I won't thank you, Vanessa!" Deepak returned and entered the bagel store.

"Good morning, Vikas!" Deepak said.

"Good morning, Deepak. How are you?" Vikas responded in Hindi as he spoke in Hindi at times. Both could understand and speak Hindi. It was the influence of Bollywood movies in their individual homelands.

"I am good. My roommate gave me a ride," he answered, putting his backpack by the register.

"That's good," he said before turning back to his work. Deepak walked into the restroom, changed into his uniform, and started working.

"Hello, sir, how are you? Can I help you?" he asked a customer.

"Yes, please, plain bagel, toasted with cream cheese, an egg and bacon."

Deepak took a plain bagel and tried to cut it in half.

"Wait, wait," Margarita stopped him. "This is how you cut a bagel." She spoke as if she was the manager of the bagel store and sliced the bagel in front of him. "You go and sweep now, I will take the order."

Deepak said nothing to her; he simply started sweeping up the crumbs. He felt like a dog when Margarita was ordering him around and old wounds once again reopened. It had been engrained in him that he was not supposed to do menial jobs like the one he was doing right now, nor should or could an uneducated person like Margarita order him around. He knew it was a sharp string of pride, but he could not let it go.

As soon as Deepak finished sweeping, Margareta told him to mop the floor. Deepak remembered an English literature class he taught in a classroom of many students while in Nepal:

Dear students, Karl Marx says that it is not the consciousness that determines the social being rather it is the social being that determines the consciousness...

What the fuck am I doing here? Deepak retorted silently as he mopped the floor and again calmed himself. He had started swearing in the word "Fuck" that he never liked before and hated Ganesh for using it. *I am doing this for my American dream.* Vikas spotted at him moping and mumbling to himself.

"How are you feeling? Vikas asked. "Are you homesick for your country or what, looks like you are mumbling?"

I was a lecturer in my country, and I am a sweeper here. Every second, my country swirls around in my mind, Deepak wanted to say, but said "No, its okay."

Don't feel bad. It'll be okay," Vikas said smiling as if he knew what Deppak was thinking of. "You know, when I came to America ten years ago, I had painful feelings that you might have now. I was a physician in Bangladesh, and I became a sweeper here. Everybody loves to work here. People don't see any work as inferior or superior. Even a professor doesn't hesitate to mop." Vikas' voice was soft and conciliatory as he turned the bacon in the pan. Customers were eating bagels sitting around the tables.

Deepak rested for a second and then continued his work, listening intently to Vikas' every word. "I cried a lot during my first days in the U.S. I tried many times to go back to my country, but later I realized that it was all going to be okay. I had to work 13 hours a day, standing on my feet. I had to carry heavy things around and provide them to customers. I had to clean tables and toilets." The bacon hissed; Vikas flipped it. "Now, I have my own house in America. I drive a Lexus car and a Camry. My standard of life has changed. You have to work hard, man." He started packing the bagels in a paper bag to go. Deepak stood holding the mop for a few seconds.

"I am okay. I don't have bad feelings," Deepak said, but Vikas could see the truth in his face.

"Bad feelings come in the beginning, you know? When you get used to it, it goes away," Vikas said. "See, a customer came. Go and take his order." Leaving the mop against the wall behind the table, Deepak washed his hands, wiped them with a paper towel, and went to take the customer's order.

"Can I help you, sir?" Deepak asked the customer. "Yes, please. I would like a plain bagel, toasted."

"Sure, sir." After Deepak toasted the bagel, he asked, "Anything else, sir?"

"Just cheese and bacon."

"Sure, sir. It is for here or to go?"

"It is for here."

Deepak cut the bagel in two halves and put cheese and bacon on it and gave it to him. The customer left and, a couple seconds later, returned to the counter.

"What's wrong with this bagel?" he asked. "Did you toast it?" the customer immediately returned to the register and complained.

"Yes sir, I toasted it," Deepak said hesitantly.

"I don't like this bagel."

"Can I make you another one, Sir?" Vikas said softly stepping into the conversation.

"Go ahead," the customer told him.

After serving the customer, Vikas explained to Deepak, "Deepak, we have to make every customer happy. That is customer service in America. Here, customer service is very important. Most of the time, it is assumed that customers are always right, so we should not argue with them even if they make a mistake."

Deepak nodded.

After working for a few hours, focused on making customers happy, Vikas announced to Deepak, "Your work is done here today. Go to Succulent Sandwiches. I will be there in half an hour."

The distance between Succulent Sandwiches and the bagel store was not far. Deepak did not see anyone walking on the street beside himself. Only cars were moving and traffic lights blinking while Deepak crossed the road. After only a few yards, the weather was cold enough to tolerate. Deepak arrived at Succulent Sandwiches, where Rita was busy serving a customer. She smiled at him.

"How are you?" she asked.

"I am fine, *Didi*" Deepak said. "How are you?"

"The same as yesterday," she replied. She was right because she was doing the same job every day, and there was nothing new.

"*Bhai*, how do you like America?" she asked him the same question she asked on the first day.

Deepak could not answer her question, and simply smiled, hiding his frustration, anxiety, and pain.

Working at Succulent Sandwiches was not easy for him. He had to stand for hours, which made his back hurt, his legs weak, and his backbone burn.

More than anything, he felt humiliated, but he hoped that would go away in time. Still, working at Succulent Sandwiches was better than working at the bagel store. There were no younger workers ordering him around, and it did not take long for him to learn how to make sandwiches. He found himself strangely satisfied to have a new skill.

"Did you eat something at the bagel store, *Bhai*?" Rita asked him.

"No," Deepak replied, his head hung low and his shoulders hunched over.

"Eat something first," she ordered. There was an advantage to working with Rita because she was from the same country and allowed him certain privileges. "Can I make a sandwich for you?" she asked.

"Okay."

"Do you eat bacon, *Bhai*?"

Deepak remembered his father's advice. " Son, do not eat any other meat except for chicken and mutton."

"What is the bacon made of?" Deepak asked.

"Pork."

"Oh, no," Deepak said. "Only chicken"

She made a chicken sandwich and handed it over to him, saying, "Eat first."

After this, she introduced him once more to different kinds of bread: Italian herb and cheese, Monterey cheddar, parmesan oregano bread, and nine-grain wheat. He tried to memorize sauces like mayonnaise, honey mustard, sweet onion, and ranch. She also taught him how to wrap sandwiches.

A few hours later, Vikas arrived at the store and sniffed, "Your duty is finished for today, come tomorrow at noon." Deepak was sweeping at that time.

Deepak looked up from sweeping the floor and paused. "If you don't mind, can I have time off tomorrow? I have a class, which I should not miss. Every Monday and Friday, I have classes. And I have a lot of assignments to do"

"Okay," Vikas said, "but if you don't come regularly, it'll take you longer to learn everything you need to know."

He was about to leave and Vikas called out, "Hey, Deepak, wait a minute. I will drop you off at your apartment since I also go home the same way."

Deepak waited half an hour for a ride home from Vikas. He didn't mind the wait because it would take him more than two hours to get home on foot, so the drive was a welcome relief.

On the way home, Vikas talked about what he considered to be the purity of his culture.

"I have a small son; I don't like him being reared here. I want him to learn about his culture and cultural behaviors," Vikas sniffed while turning off the air conditioner, making it a bit warmer in the car. "After five years, I will go back to my country and live there until I breathe my last breath." Deepak continued nodding his head in approval and kept saying "that's right!"

Vikas dropped off Deepak near the apartment complex entrance so he didn't have to navigate his way back out. Tired, Deepak showered quickly, changed into a t-shirt and shorts, lay across his bed, and began thinking of his family and people back home. Memories of life in Nepal chased one each other in an unrelenting game in his head.

"If all Nepali people did their jobs without feeling superior or inferior, my country would also develop," Deepak wrote in his diary that was lying by the pillow in his bed. His eyes grew as heavy as his body felt and he slowly drifted off to sleep.

Melissa came to him in his sleep. He smiled looking at her beautiful face. He thought of her caring personality, and pictured how she said "goodbye."

Chapter 12: Birthday

It was the month of December, freezing outside. Melissa was off to Texas to visit her parents and celebrate Christmas there. All the trees were bare and the branches were hanging low. The sky was a clear, azure blue. Some crows, the neighborhood road-kill disposal experts, were cawing, which was not a good omen. "Why are you cawing, crows?" Deepak questioned aloud, turning toward the crows' incessant noise that blared through the window. In Nepal, it was said that if crows caw, it is a sign of a bad message they have brought. "Tell me the message you have brought from Nepal," he talked to the crows outside the window. The crows became silent.

Deepak wondered if something terrible had happened back in his homeland. He tried to call his parents, but he could not get through. The line kept disconnecting. "The number you have dialed cannot be completed at this time," a computer lady's voice spoke into his phone.

"Fuck," Deepak mumbled throwing the phone on the floor. This was the second time he had used the swearing word "fuck."

Despite his concern, Deepak still had to go to work. He ate a quick breakfast, a peanut butter and jelly sandwich, and put on a heavy jacket he bought from Nepal rushed the two miles on foot to the bagel store.

Customers were lined up to purchase bagels. Vikas, Margareta, and Daniel were already very busy making bagels, ringing up the customers' purchases, and scrambling and frying eggs.

"Good morning, Vikas," Deepak chirped despite his exhaustion, taking off the jacket and hanging by the wall. It was warmer inside due to the heating. Heating in

99

cold weather and AC in warm weather was available everywhere.

"Morning," Vikas replied curtly without looking up. "Go and take that customer's order. Do it quickly!"

"Alright," Deepak said, jumping into action.

"Put gloves on, first."

"Alright."

"Don't forget to say, 'Welcome to Sunny Bagel' to the customers."

"Alright."

Deepak followed Vikas' orders like an army battalion in command.

"Now you have been working for a month, you must know this job for yourself. Nobody is going to teach you because nobody has enough time to teach you," Vikas told him in a commanding voice. Deepak just remained silent. He felt tired and the line on his forehead puckered.

"Do you hear me?" Vikas said, looking at Deepak. Such a soft and seemingly kind hearted person all of a sudden sounded harsh.

"Alright," Deepak said through his teeth, taming his frustration and putting gloves on before going to grab bagels for a customer.

"You should have learned some of this stuff in a few days, but you have not learned yet. You know, you have been working for a while now. You are very slow. Try to be quick," Vikas sniffed. "I don't like a slow person."

"I am doing my best, Vikas," Deepak answered, amassing the courage to speak to him. His hands were trembling and legs were shaking. He could not understand why his whole body trembled.

"Okay, go and bring some slices of turkey from the cooler," Vikas ordered.

"Sure, sir." Deepak went to the cooler to fetch a turkey breast, but he did not know where it was kept.

He looked around for them in the cooler. It was so cold that he felt as if he was frozen. He hugged himself to feel warmth in his body and spent a few minutes trying to find the turkey breasts. He moved the different stuff in the cooler so he could find what he was looking for, but to no avail. He came out of the cooler shivering. Vikas easily spotted his empty hands.

"I don't see it," Deepak admitted.

"What?" Vikas spat. Deepak saw the veins on Vikas' neck swelling and bulging. Vikas sniffed even louder.

"I couldn't find it," Deepak repeated. His voice trembled with fear.

Vikas took off his plastic gloves and threw them into the dustbin forcefully. He rushed toward Deepak as if he was going to slap him. "What are you doing here? You don't even know where the turkey breasts are, and you have been working for more than enough time. I am not happy with you," Vikas said sternly. "Come with me. I will show you." With that, he entered the cooler with Deepak at his heels. He grabbed the turkey breasts off the shelf, saying, "Look. What is this? You need to have proper eyes to see them." Vikas came out with the turkey breasts and left Deepak inside the cooler, saying, "Bring the rest."

Deepak felt suddenly ashamed and embarrassed. Vikas had a right to be mad. Tears of embarrassment welled up in his eyes. He was ashamed that he had failed at such a simple task. A couple of months prior, he would have felt that Vikas was rude and uncouth. Now, he just felt upset for disappointing the other man. His head whirled. He wanted to crush himself into the cooler in shame.

Who is here to hear my feelings, to understand what is going on in my life? Deepak complained.

He came out with the rest of the turkey breasts and brought them to the oven before he fled to the sanctuary of the restroom. There, he shut the door and started hiccupping. He looked into the mirror, touching the swollen eyes and wiping the rolling tears. He felt lost but strangely relieved.

He remembered the director of his program who recommended that he return home if he had no money. He remembered the director of International Student Admissions who also advised him to go home. He knew that was not his goal. His goal was to pursue the American dream.

At least Vikas was paying him. He decided to continue such work. "I will have my golden future after a year or two," he talked to himself wiping his tears using the paper towel in the bathroom. After that, he forced a smile onto his lips and tried to work as fast as he could. He helped customers, and fried eggs, bacon and sausages. He swept and mopped.

Vikas approached him. His eyes concealed rage and sympathy at the same time. After Deepak finished mopping, Vikas spoke gruffly but softly, "You can go home now; the next time, try to work faster. Be quicker."

Deepak did not say anything. He just nodded and left the bagel store, picking his backpack off a table. One of his co-workers had told him about a bus route he could take, so he tried it out.

It was so freezing outside that even his thick jacket could not handle it. He shivered and started waiting for the bus at the station. After a few minutes the bus arrived. He had figured out that the bus started in the morning at 7 and ran until 7 P.M., except for weekends, via the route of his apartment. *How nice it would have been if I knew about that way before*, Deepak spoke to himself. It was his first time riding on a bus. He had to pay a dollar bill. He felt very relaxed and comfortable as he stared out of the bus window.

The world looked open and free; trees in the horizon circled around. Different languages hummed

102

around the bus.

Deepak got off at his stop and went back to the apartment. He entered his living room and took a nap until it turned evening. As he woke up, he noticed the light was turned off, replaced by candles. The room was filled with perfume. Vanessa came out of her bedroom, and then Lucas. Then they both yelled, "Happy birthday!"

"Oh!" Deepak laughed in delight. "How did you know that today was my birthday?" He had completely forgotten it himself. "You guys surprised me!"

"We found it, *Deepak*. We found it," Vanessa teased, hitting her fist on her palm.

"Please tell me how did you know?" Deepak insisted. "I never had a birthday celebration in my life. You guys really made my night awesome." Deepak's tiredness vanished like vapor; instead, he felt very jovial and excited.

"We checked on your Facebook profile and found it," Lucas said. Deepak had recently opened a Facebook account. Facebook had started becoming one of the most used social media after it came into existence in 2004 when Mark Zuckerberg founded it.

"You guys are unbelievable," Deepak said, a smile glued to his face. "Thank you so much, Lucas. Thank you so much, Vanessa! How lucky I am to have such wonderful roommates!"

"You're welcome, Deepak," Vanessa and Lucas said.

There was a blue and white cake for him, and they took photographs of him seated behind it. Deepak blew out the four candles they had placed on it, wishing for a good future as they sang "happy birthday to you" while clapping. The three of them ate cake and posed for pictures.

That night, Deepak fell asleep as soon as his head hit the pillow, the worries of the day forgotten.

Chapter 13: Illness

Deepak could not get up in the morning. He had trouble opening his eyes. His forehead was hot to the touch, and cold and clammy at times. His lips looked rough and cracked uneven and very dry; he tried to clear his throat as if he felt sand in it. He struggled out of bed and made his way to the bathroom. His morning ritual took him longer than usual. He found a thermometer in the cabinet drawers and, a few moments later, he knew he got a fever. He took the thermometer to measure his temperature. It was 102 degrees. The confirmation only made him feel sicker. Weakly, he stumbled back to sofa. He realized he could not get up from the bed now, even if he wanted. *How can I make it to work today?* he talked to himself. He continued to lie on the bed staring at the ceiling.

In a while, Vanessa emerged from her bedroom and made her way to the kitchen. Seeing Deepak awake, she called as she walked, "Good morning, Deepak. How are you?" She was not expecting anything from Deepak but "I am fine."

"I am not feeling well, Vanessa. I have a fever," he said, touching his forehead with his palm.

"Oh, no! Working and walking so long a route every day in such cold weather out there might have made you sick, Deepak. You need to take a rest," she chided, coming closer to Deepak and touching his forehead. Her hands on his forehead briefly relieved Deepak, perhaps he thought those hands were Melissa's or his mother at home.

"I have to go to work this morning, but I can't. I have to call Vikas to let him know that I'm sick, but I don't have the courage to tell him. I don't want him to be mad," he said, sounding like a child afraid of certain punishment.

"Why don't I call him for you?" she asked, taking her cell phone out of her pocket.

"Thank you," he said, relieved, and gave her the phone number.

After a quick phone call, she hung up and said, "Vikas said it is alright." Her words offered a measure of comfort. "Now, don't worry. Just take a rest; everything will be fine. Did you eat something this morning?"

"I have no appetite, Vanessa," he said, tossing to the other side of the sofa.

"No, you should eat something, *Deepak*. What do you like to eat? I can cook for you."

"I feel like not eating anything right now," he said.

"Look, Deepak, in the U.S., there are no people to take care of you. You have to take care of yourself. If you don't eat, your health is going to be even worse. No one can afford to get sick here. I'm training to be a nurse, remember? I know the cost of health care. If you don't look after yourself, you're just going to get worse." Vanessa lectured as she made her way to the kitchen. "I understand your problems. Don't hesitate to tell me what you like. I'm like your sister." *You are more like a beloved to me*, Deepak mused. Still, Deepak would not refuse her sisterly love.

"I guess noodles don't sound bad," Deepak offered, rubbing his tongue over his dry lips.

"Okay, I'll pick up some noodles from the gas station. If Lucas asks where I went, tell him that I went to buy a phone card," she said, then smiled. "Sometimes, he's an asshole, you know? But I love him anyway."

Deepak nodded his head half in acknowledgement and half in approval of her evaluation of her boyfriend. As she reached for her car keys, he drew the blanket over his head and turned to face the wall.

Sleep must have been near since Vanessa

returned in what seemed like a minute with noodles from the gas station and microwaved them for him.

"Deepak, here you go," she handed the cup of noodles over to him. "After you finish eating, take a rest. If you need something, just let me know."

"Sure, Vanessa," Deepak said. "Thank you so much." He felt his voice shake and his hands tremble as he held the warm noodles.

"No problem, Deepak." Vanessa returned to the kitchen. Deepak ate the soup and noodles and slept. Eventually, Lucas surfaced from the bedroom. "What's going on?" he asked, noticing that Deepak had not gone to work.

"Baby, Deepak is very sick," Vanessa spoke softly, looking toward Deepak and back again to her boyfriend.

"Oh, really?" Lucas sounded indifferent and stretched toward his girlfriend. He kissed her, an early morning kiss perhaps, not giving a glance in Deepak's direction. Vanessa clung to Lucas and both of them disappeared into their bedroom.

Oh lord, I lost a day's wages. But what could I do? Deepak murmured tossing and turning in his bed. The sofa was his bed.

Chills racked Deepak's body and his mind gave him no rest. Reasoning with himself, he argued that there was nothing more important than his health. *Am not I really too sick to go to work?* he questioned to himself, coughing and holding his chest as if it was hurting him while coughing.

Finding it hard now to lift his head from the pillow, he reached for his ever-present friend, the laptop, and started listening to Nepali music online: *Yeklai basda sandai malai samjana timro aaidinchha sahana nasaki ankha bata ansu tesai jharidinchha—"I remember you all the time when I am alone and I cannot prevent my tears from rolling down my cheeks."*

His eyes filled with tears. Rolling his tongue

around his mouth, he attempted to induce a flow of saliva and wet his lips with the little that was produced. His teeth chattered as a wave of coldness followed by heat enveloped his body. It had been a few days since he spoke to Melissa. He pictured her in his imagination, sitting by him rubbing his back and caressing his hair.

However, she was not there. She had not arrived back in the state from her Christmas leave. The college was closed for Christmas holiday. The first semester was over and the second one would start soon in January. *If Melissa was here, perhaps she would come see me*, he thought silently.

A jumble of mumbled words escaped his mouth and, in moments of lucidity, he felt helplessness and anger, followed by tears. Books were strewn around on the table, under the bed, and he had become quite attached to a couple of them. Salman Rushdie's *Midnight's Children*, and *Mimic Man* by V. S. Naipaul held the privilege of sitting beside his bed.

Deepak reached for Mimic Man and his fingers flipped through the pages. Mimic Man, the novel of cultural displacement, masterfully evokes the colonial man's experience in a postcolonial world. Deepak also knew how writing gave Ralph Sing, the character in the novel, order in his chaotic existence. Midnight's Children deals with India's transition from British colonialism to independence and partition of India.

These two books always fascinated Deepak. He always loved the post-colonial theories to understand how European/westerners or rich countries exert power over the easterners or poor countries and define the poor, the marginalized through their knowledge. In the line, he remembered another two names Edward Said, his orientalism, and Michael Foucault, his concept of truth and power. Deepak wondered if his American dream could be an illusion.

Writing and Reading was impossible for Deepak

107

now. Weakly he threw the book toward the table; it missed. Deepak tossed and turned on his sofa-bed as his breathing came fast and shallow. He tried to breathe normally and felt himself gasping for air whenever he moved. He closed his eyes, but sleep eluded him. *Be optimistic, be optimistic!* He repeated the words like a mantra. He smiled blankly and vaguely.

He again remembered Melissa. He liked her, her eyes, her caring personality, her presence in class and her look. He grabbed his diary and wrote about Melissa picturing her.

> *I had never felt the absence of you before*
> *Because I never knew who you were.*
> *You stopped by me and offered me a generous heart,*
> *So lovely, so kindly, so tenderly.*
> *You touched my heart in such a way that*
> *I started feeling the rhythm of your heart in my heart,*
> *Started overhearing the music of your musing,*
> *So calm, so soothing, so appeasing.*
> *My body and soul became yoked together in your name.*
> *You were looking for the same person I was looking for,*
> *Upright, benevolent, trustworthy.*
> *You doubted what I doubted Adultery, hypocrisy, snobbery.*
> *There you go—the same feeling, same dreams, same desire,*
> *We wanted to spread our lives together.*
> *So intimacy grew like the rushing of a mountain river*
> *Which never dries unless mountains cease to exist,*
> *Or the stars, or the moon, or the sun fails to exist.*
> *When I remember you I do not see smoke swaddling the sky,*
> *Nor I feel the harsh wind blowing outside.*
> *What I see is that birds are free, creatures are unfettered,*
> *Prisoners are unchained.*
> *Day follows night silently, stealthily, playfully,*
> *For a wonderful daybreak.*
> *I wish you could be sitting next to me right know*
> *So I could touch your hands and play*
> *With the lines on your palm,*
> *Fixing the fate and future of our life.*

He felt hungry. He had not finished eating the noodles Vanessa gave to him earlier and that was sitting on the side. It was turned too cold and sitting there for too long to eat now. He slowly walked into the kitchen, talking to himself and dumping the noodles into the sink. He opened the door of the refrigerator. The contents of it were uninteresting, and he returned to his sofa-bed. The apartment was deadly quiet apart from the low hum of the refrigerator and the intermittent drone of the air-conditioning. Perhaps Lucas and Vanessa had gone out. Perhaps they had exhausted each other, as usual, and were sleeping.

Vanessa appeared over him suddenly and asked, "How's your fever, Deepak? Can I get you something?"

"I think it is still bad, I'm still feeling hot and cold at the same time." His hoarse voice and the beads of perspiration that lined his forehead agreed.

"You need more rest," she sounded motherly. "Do you want to eat something else?"

"No, thank you."

"Are you worried about your health?"

"No, Vanessa."

"Good. Don't worry. Worries will make you worse."

"I am okay"

"If you need anything, please tell me," Vanessa said with a smile and disappeared back in her bedroom. Deepak turned once again to face the wall and tried to sleep. However, he could not sleep mulling over financial constraints, not being able to go to work and thinking of another semester and its tuition fee, and parents back home. He missed home even more. He realized home is deeply missed in a foreign land when one becomes sick.

Chapter 14: Memories

Deepak was still lying on the sofa, his fever remained the same. Outside the window, snow blizzards fell on the cars on the parking lot and the dried boughs of the trees hanging low. Deepak never saw the snow live in front of him before. *It's beautiful.* Just looking outside, he felt his fever lessened. Squirrels had disappeared to hibernate. His memories in the rented room back in Kathmandu surfaced.

A car passes by his rented-room, honking its horn. A noisy motorcycle rushes by, hooting without a muffler. The trash collector follows behind him, going door-to-door. Teenagers travel the same lane, discussing, arguing, and wrangling with foul words in loud voices. Just opposite the house where Deepak lives, a bulldozer and concrete mixer shrieks, hurting his ears. In a fit of anger, Deepak beats his fist against the wall, shouting, slamming the window.

The houses in America were systematically constructed. The apartments were in areas zoned for residential use only. The personal apartments were built far from downtown. In Nepal, everything was chaotic.

Kathmandu, his home of a few years, was a disturbing and distressful place. The mushrooming buildings were constructed haphazardly, without any real zoning. A concrete jungle now occupied every open lot. There was no proper place for a recreation field or playground.

America was a welcome respite, a place he was running toward. From the window of his U.S. apartment, Deepak could see a tennis court and swimming pool. In most apartment complexes, he had heard they had a gym. These things were only dreams in Nepal. In the

U.S., street vendors did not cry out to sell their products, nor did trash collectors shout their arrival as they moved into the neighborhood.

Deepak reached for the thermometer lying next to him and took his temperature. It was the same, a steady 102 degrees. He wondered why the fever had not left. Memories of his family visited him.

Family and friends gather to meet him. Hot spicy tea greets each visitor. People come uninvited and linger for days. Lying down on his childhood bed, his parents hang over him, concerned about his health. His mother brings some medicine and gives him a cup of water. His father puts a wet cloth on his forehead to reduce his temperature.

He remembered what his mother had told him what the doctor said when he was in his mother's belly, "I am not sure whether I can save the mother's life."

Deepak could not stop thinking. Deepak surfaced back to his reality. He was unable to work. Without work, nothing worked. Little by little, his dreams appeared to be slipping out of his grasp. He felt hot one minute then cold; every bone seemed to ache in a way he continued mumbling the pain. Water leaked from his pores and drenched the sheets, sweat trickled in his face. More than anything, Deepak longed for the touch of someone familiar, someone that knew and would understand how he felt. He missed the comfort of speaking in Nepali. He found himself whispering, "Oh, God please help me!"

He imagined Vanessa followed by Melissa coming to check his temperature. She brought lukewarm water and helped him drink it. She massaged his back. She put a blanket over him, kissed his forehead, and left the room, saying, "If you need anything, just call for me." He knew Vanessa was not there, nor Melissa.

Again, Deepak felt for the thermometer and checked his temperature. It was still high. *Will I die*

111

from this fever or what? Deepak's lips felt rough to the touch of his fingers. *Would this fever cost me my life before my parents see me again?* Deepak's eyes shut. *What about my American dream?* He daydreamed: *he becomes a professor at Harvard. He drives a BMW 7 series. He signs books at a table and a line of people as far as the eye could see clutched a copy of his latest book. Reporters from CNN, NBC, and FOX swarm around him. Lights flash, cameras roll. People shout his name. He smiles up at the crowd as he looks at his star on the Hollywood Walk of Fame.*

He opened his eyes.

"A little fever is not going to kill me. I won't die so easily without fulfilling my dreams," Deepak said aloud as he lay in a pool of his own sweat.

"Life is so short, and no one can be sure when they will die," he remembered what his grandmother said, while cooking in the kitchen.

His uncle, stationed in Iraq, sits beside him and smiles at Deepak. "To achieve a goal, each person has their choice, for which there must be dedication, devotion, and meditation," his uncle said. "To reach the summit of success, one should not be overcome by emotions."

All those people's voices echoed in his sleep. Deepak's mind raced. The bed still held him captive. "I will learn from you, uncle." Deepak whispered. "I will be optimistic."

"How to be optimistic?" he questioned again. Deepak held to the belief, that everything was a part and parcel of human life: sorrow and happiness, sweet and bitter, life and death. With that in mind, life only seemed to be more splendid and meaningful. It was better to take pleasure in what he had than to delve deeper into the bitter reality of life. The search for truth and reality made his life more painful and pathetic, agonizing and wretched in his sickbed.

112

Chapter 15: Feeling better

A week passed. When he woke up, his fever broke. Hours passed and he began to feel a little better. *Thanks, God I was sick during the college holiday, otherwise I would miss many classes and assignments,* he whispered to himself. Turning over on his side, he managed to swing his feet over the side of the sofa-bed and push himself up with his hands. Someone had placed a bottle of water on the table. He took a few sips and returned to bed and his restless slumber. Vanessa's keys clicked as she entered the apartment, and he opened his eyes to see that she had a bundle of letters in her hand.

"How's your fever, Deepak?" she asked, handing him a letter. "Here's your mail."

"I think it will be better," Deepak croaked.

"Let me check your temperature," she said and went to her room and returned with a disposable thermometer.

Deepak opened the envelope Vanessa had given him. It was nothing but an advertisement for car insurance. Deepak discarded the letter. He picked up the laptop and checked his email instead. His sister had written an email:

Hello brother,

We miss you a lot. How are you doing? Take care of yourself. Our love and good wishes are always with you. Our parents feel very lonely since you left us. They feel your absence though they talk to you on the phone. Since you left us, I wish I also could be with you and study at the same university where you are studying. At every breakfast, lunch, and dinner, we remember you. Our mom's eyes become teary and I also cannot stop tears from rolling down my face.

113

Your sister

Moist eyes replied to his sister's words and he sniffed. Vanessa stood over him.

"What's the matter, *Nino*?" she asked. "Is the fever hurting you?" she asked.

"No, I'm okay," Deepak replied, trying to wipe his tears.

"Don't worry. Everything will be fine, Deepak," she comforted, taking his temperature and blood pressure.

"Oh, you're getting better. It is only 99 degrees now," she smiled and she left for the kitchen where she warmed up a cup of instant soup for him. Deepak thanked her and drank it, relishing the gesture and the comfort it provided his body, before he went back to sleep.

He had been off many days from work. It was a great financial loss, but he tried not to think too hard about it. He knew worrying would do him no good, not when his whole body was still aching.

Chapter 16: Vanessa Leaves

Deepak felt a lot better. He got to the bagel store early; there were four cars already parked outside. Customers were inside, eating bagels stuffed with cream cheese.

"Good morning, Vikas," Deepak called out to his boss cheerily as he entered the store.

"Oh, *Bhaisap*, what's up?" Vikas sniffed. "How're you now? Are you feeling better?"

"I'm good, a lot better" Deepak said. "I recovered from the fever, but I'm still feeling a little dizzy though." Deepak realized he could not stand for very long, but he knew he should pretend he could work hard. "I'm alright, though, ready to do anything."

"Okay. You gotta sweep first," Vikas said, pointing to the area in and around the cooler.

"Yes, sir," Deepak said, looking for a broom.

As Deepak started to sweep, hunger and thirst assaulted him at the same time. He reached into the refrigerator, took a bottle of water out, and began to drink it.

"Do you know those bottles in the refrigerator are for sale? They are not for you. You gotta pay for that," Vikas' voice rose, as he glowered and sniffed in anger.

"Sorry," Deepak said. "I didn't know that." The sudden tension and cold water caused his heart to race, making his head throb severely. He felt dizzy and fell to the floor.

"Oh, my God," Vikas cried out. "Are you okay?" He held Deepak's hands and helped him stand up. Since there were not any customers around to see him falling, Vikas tried to manage to support him.

"Yes, I am. I just felt very dizzy," Deepak said,

touching his temple.

"If you're not well, you can go home. Take a rest," he said.

His face turned red. He was afraid he might have to pay for Deepak's treatment if he became seriously ill at the store. On top of that, he was an illegal worker. If one of the customers called an ambulance, there was no telling what trouble they might all be in.

"It's okay. I can work," Deepak struggled to stand. The mantra "no work, no life" played in his head. Fees, food, family, rent all swam around his eyes. He had to work.

"If you cannot work, tell me. I will hire another person," Vikas gave words to his Deepak's unspoken fear.

"No, no, I can work. This is just the fever. It has gone, but I am a little weak. I will be okay by tomorrow."

"Please let me know if you can't work," Vikas nodded hesitantly, trying to reassure himself as well as Deepak.

"I think I can work, Vikas."

"Are you sure?" Vikas shook his head with misgiving. "If you want to go home, let me know, I will drop you off." Going home did sound nice.

Finally, Deepak nodded his head in approval. He got into the car relieved as Vikas drove deftly through the morning traffic to take him home.

When Deepak opened the door of the apartment and entered, he heard the sound of crying. Vanessa was sobbing on the couch with her face in her hands. Lucas was nowhere to be seen.

"What's the matter, Vanessa?" Deepak softly asked. "Why are you crying?"

She ran over to him at the door, held him tightly, and cried until Deepak felt like crying.

"What's wrong with you, Vanessa?" Deepak's mind raced over a million and one possibilities, frantic

116

with worry. "Why are you crying so hard?" He asked as he rubbed her back. She reminded him of his little sister, running to him for consolation after falling down.

"I gave everything to Lucas—my life, my happiness, my promise—but he broke my heart," she gulped and tears ran down her face. The whole apartment echoed with her terrible wailing.

"What happened, Vanessa?" he said, genuinely surprised and puzzled. "I thought that you two were in a committed relationship. I can't imagine you two breaking up."

Vanessa cried even more bitterly, hiding her head on his chest. Deepak kept holding her, caressed her head, and wiped her tears with his hands. She broke free, stood, and sniffed, finally able to speak. "I found texts that Lucas had sent to another woman," she said, shaking her head wildly. Her hair became disheveled. A flood of tears fell from her eyes. Her eyes were swollen, and her lips had dried. Deepak felt helpless.

"Are you sure?" he asked trying to salvage something to give her hope. He could not bear to see her in this state. "Maybe there is some explanation."

"No, no. I'm sure."

Deepak was dumbstruck. He remembered how passionately they were in love. He remembered the relentless kisses, her twirling around in Lucas' arms, the coy looks. Now, everything seemed to have turned sour in an instant.

"Did you talk with Lucas?"

"Yes, I talked to him." "What did he say?"

"He said he wrote those texts just for fun. That it didn't mean anything."

"Then why don't you believe him?"

"I can't, Deepak," she said. "I called the number and some woman said that she was Lucas's girlfriend and told me to "fuck off." She said that they have been an item for three months. I thought it was just my imagination. I can't live here anymore, I need to leave this room and go away. My parents don't know I'm living with a boyfriend here in the U.S. They think that I'm just studying hard. They would be so mad...I don't want to hurt them. I liked Lucas, I thought we were going to get married, but he deceived me."

"No, Vanessa...Try to talk to him. You need to know the truth." He still felt dizzy, like he was reeling.

"No, I can't," Vanessa said, moving further away.

Deepak walked over to her and pulled her toward him. She was still crying and clung to him like a baby. As he held her closely, he felt the beat of her heart and the warmth of her skin.

His imagination took over. He was kissing her eyes and she was kissing him. They fell in a crumpled heap on the floor and their hands began searching each other's bodies for comfort. He lost all sense of what he was doing. He felt her warm breath on his skin. His fingers became entangled in her hair, her breasts and the sweet, moist softness that she had only shared with Lucas.

He realized that he was getting carried away with his daydreaming and hoped that she had not sensed that his mind had wandered. Vanessa was still sobbing, and he was unable to pacify her. He held her silently until her tears subsided. Eventually, she broke free from him and went to her room. Deepak heard her weeping quietly.

Sometime later, she returned to the living room, suitcases in hand, and walked over and hugged him. "Good-bye, Deepak," she murmured, "I will be in touch. You can use my laptop, I don't need it." The smile on her lips did not reach her eyes. With that, she left.

Deepak felt awful. She was the one who had welcomed him, who took care of him. He was going to miss her. The house felt empty without her warmth. There would be no one to give him even a glass of water in case he became sick, no one to comfort him selflessly.

Lucas returned to the house later that night with a friend and only offered Deepak a small greeting. He found it hard to look Lucas in the eye. Deepak hated Lucas for what he had done to Vanessa.

"Did you see Vanessa?" Lucas finally asked Deepak when they were alone.

"She's gone for good." Deepak caressed the sad thought in his mind.

He went to bed, his mind was in turmoil. As he lay down on the bed, Vikas phoned him.

"Deepak," he said, his voice heavy, "I'm sorry. I hired another person. I need a strong person who can work for long hours. If you become very sick while working at my store, I can't take care of you." After a pause, Vikas added, "Come tomorrow to get your money."

Deepak broke into an immediate sweat. Words worked up in his throat and got stuck there. "No, Vikas, I'm strong. I can really work well."

"It's okay. Please, try another job."

"Don't say that, Vikas, please," Deepak begged uselessly.

His tears wet the pillow. His stomach hurt and his chest burned. In his head he would do the same in Vikas' shoes, but, in his heart, he felt sick. The next semester was almost there and he had to pay the tuition fee immediately.

Deepak hung up the phone, his head burning. "America is not the land of opportunity, but the land of selfishness, money-minded people and capitalism!" Deepak murmured. First Lucas, now Vikas.

Deepak silently cried in pain, tossing and turning over in his sofa-bed. He had gone through so much to stay in America, but it had done nothing for him. The American Dream that the movies sold was all fiction. *I hate America!* He threw the pillow. He pummeled his bed until his fists hurt. He was angry with himself, but America was an easy target to blame.

What the hell have I done to deserve this? All I wanted was a tiny bit of the dream that you'd enticed me with. Where is my portion of the dream? Deepak continued rambling.

Chapter 17: Nepali Party

It was the last day of December. Deepak's 6 months in America had passed. Christmas had come and gone like any other day for Deepak. *Melissa will be there soon for the spring semester,* he thought. It had been more than a month since he met and spoke to Melissa on campus and at his apartment parking-lot. That was the last "bye," "see you soon," and "Merry Christmas" in advance. She never called him, nor did Deepak. Deepak had his own issues and didn't bother with calling her. Perhaps, he gave her space to enjoy her family time. He realized how big and important the festivals are.

He was at home alone, jobless. Lucas had been away since Christmas Eve. Deepak took up a book from the table and tried to read, but he was too distracted. The phone rang, breaking his thoughts.

"Hey Deepak," said a voice on the other end. "This is Ganesh. How're you? Want to go to a New Year's party tonight? Many Nepali people gather there."

"A party sounds nice," he said, relieved to have an interruption to his solitary confinement, "but I have to look for a job, brother."

"What happened to the job in the bagel store?"

"I lost it."

"Shit!" Ganesh sounded truly shocked. "Don't worry. We'll look for another job, then. I'll help you. Tomorrow. Tonight, we're going to the party."

The opportunity to get out the apartment to meet other Nepalese people filled him with excitement. Deepak hurriedly showered and pulled out a pair of dress pants, and a shirt he had never worn. In less than fifteen minutes, he was ready.

Right on time, Ganesh arrived to pick him up.

Leaving all his problems in the apartment, Deepak sat in the front seat of his car. Ganesh played American music at full blast.

"Don't you have Nepali songs?" Deepak asked. "Yes, I do, but I don't like Nepali songs," he said.

If it had been any other Nepali, Deepak would have been shocked, but this was Ganesh.

"There are many Nepalese songs which are very beautifully sung and very pleasing," Deepak said wishing he could play a Nepali song.

"Yes, I know. Try to listen to English songs, man," Ganesh retorted with his hands on the steering wheel and the eyes on the road. With that, he started singing along to the song on the stereo. Deepak could not trace even a single word of the song.

As they drove along, Deepak noticed that the Christmas decorations that had brightened many of the houses were all gone. As soon as the 25th turned into the 26th, discarded Christmas trees littered yards and the multicolored lights were laid to rest for another year. The residential streets that they drove through were largely deserted, except for a couple o f groups of friends looking for a party to ring in the New Year and the lovers, strolling hand in hand, exchanging kisses under lamplights. At one corner, a reckless partier vomited up his New Year's feast.

It seemed people everywhere were talking about New Year's resolutions. Politics dominated the airwaves, but commercialism anchored every discussion. The billboards that they passed advertised lawyers and churches, food, education, and plastic surgery, which seemed to sum up the lives and desires of Americans. Miracle creams and diet infomercials juxtaposed the news of the coming inauguration of the first African-American president. Every now and then, they drove past a bumper-sticker touting *McCain and Palin*, reminding Deepak that he was in a "red state," whatever

122

that meant. Deepak could not vote, and it did not seem to affect him who won the election.

Deepak's mind wondered to focus on what the next few hours would bring. Hopefully, the party would be a way to forget the past year and look forward to the New Year. *It was going to be a good year,* he told himself. He was going to make sure it was good.

The car halted in front of a building that might have been a church or school. Deepak heard music coming from the building and saw a number of people walking up the steps to the entrance. The women were decked out in saris and jewelry that shimmered in the darkness, the men, in suits, jeans, and jackets, while the children in American football jerseys and fussy pink nylon dresses scuttled behind their parents.

As Deepak and Ganesh entered, they exchanged greetings and introduced themselves to the other partygoers. The party was in full swing. Men and women took bottles of beer in their hands and celebrated the New Year with swigs of alcohol. Deepak was also offered a bottle of beer, but he refused because he wanted to look sober. He drank beer occasionally, mindful that the idea that drinking alcohol was not deemed intelligent back in Nepal.

"It is America, man!" Ganesh said. "Drink, drink."

At the party, Deepak saw people without any barrier of age, race, and sex; they hugged and kissed each other like family. Nepali, Hindi, and English songs played loudly. Some people were drunk while others danced wildly. Deepak was not a frequent partygoer, even in Nepal. He only enjoyed going to parties with people that he knew and even then, he remained a passive observer at such events.

The Nepalese Association had organized the dance party, inviting all Nepali people living in Georgia. Nepalese artistes performed to entertain and keep

123

people's spirits high. Deepak could see more than three hundred Nepalese faces: young and elderly, women and men, bachelors and spinsters.

The hall was oval-shaped, decorated with different rainbow colored lights, flashing on and off. The walls were mirrored and made the crowd seem twice as big. The hall echoed with loud music, beyond the bearing of his eardrums. The attendants in the hall were hugging, kissing, eating, dancing, singing, and drinking.

Deepak introduced himself to a few people. One was living in the U.S. on a student visa and working at a restaurant to earn money to pay tuition fees. Another was on a business visa for five years and was now a permanent resident in the U.S. after marrying an African American woman. The next was living on a diversity visa and had been living with his family for ten years in America. Some of them were government officials back in Nepal, while others were physicians, lawyers, and teachers. Most of them were working either at restaurants, gas stations, or stores like Succulent Sandwiches. Now, they were accustomed to sweeping, mopping, and washing dishes, which they had never even touched throughout their lives back in Nepal. They were doing the jobs that they thought inferior, or that only the "lower caste" people did in Nepal.

The education they earned in Nepal has nothing to do with the jobs they were doing in the U.S. However, America had its own advantages. They had their personal cars to drive along wide lanes and without many traffic jams or gas shortages. They could live in air-conditioned rooms with 24-hour electricity. They could form their own opinions about the president of America's stance on U.S. economy rather than suffer the political imbroglio and bickering politicians in Nepal.

In the U.S., they never had to confront "strikes" and "burning tires," common Nepalese tools of protest. They could send their surplus money back to their

124

families in Nepal. Though the work they were doing in the U.S. was "frustrating" and "disgusting" compared to the work they did back in Nepal, they were not only happy here, but also proud to live in America.

Deepak could see the mix of Nepali and American culture in their lifestyles. They wore ties, coats, pants and Nepali *topis,* caps. A few young women wore mini-skirts, tight shirts, and stiletto-heeled shoes, showing their cleavage. They hugged, kissed, and exchanged pleasantries. They drank and used foul language with their colleagues. They danced. A husband danced with his wife. A daughter danced with her father. A son danced with his mother. It was like a complete carnival. They seemed to forget the sense of belongingness, social status, and age differences that held them captive in Nepal.

They looked jovial and happy. Their boisterous laughter surpassed the volume of the loud speakers. They forgot reality. They forgot what Nepali politicians were doing. They forgot that more than one million Nepali people who were living on $25 per month. They forgot how many people lost their lives for the dawn of democracy in Nepal. They forgot Nepali martyrs, Nepali mothers, and Nepali mud. They forgot the dishes they washed at the restaurants during the daytime. They forgot tomorrow. They forgot everything and enjoyed the party.

Deepak saw the gathering in the hall as the manifestation of their pain. They drowned their pains with drinks and snacks. They stifled their sorrows and frustrations with dance. They hid their latent desires and dreams in their dress. It was the gathering of collective pain, which they could assuage through the forgetfulness of everything they had and would have. Inside the hall, it looked for a moment like an enactment of the true lives of Nepali immigrants in the US.

At midnight, all gathered and opened dozens of

Coronas, shook them, and sprayed them all over each other. They took a shower in beer in celebration of a happy New Year. Shortly after that, Ganesh and Deepak left the party.

They drove back via Atlanta downtown. It was a big city with skyscrapers glazed with lights. Ganesh showed him the CNN headquarter building and revolving hotel on the 90th floor. All looked mesmerizing and spellbinding. "Wow, it's amazing!" Deepak said out loud. He had never been around that area since he came to the USA. He felt lucky enough to have Ganesh to give him a tour despite the rudeness in his talk.

Ganesh dropped him off at his apartment and left.

Once he got home, Deepak felt oddly satisfied and collapsed in bed tired but happy for the first time in a while.

Chapter 18: Balloon Animals

When Deepak woke up, he still felt dizzy and slightly nauseous from the previous night's party. The first thought that surfaced in his head was: *I don't have a job.* He got up, showered, and dressed. He peeped into the other bedroom, but he was the only one home. Silence prevailed. Vanessa was gone. Lucas had become the invisible man. Deepak did not even know in whose name the apartment was rented. *Someone would come. It is not my responsibility.* He did not bother with that.

Finally, he telephoned David, the student from Uzbekistan who also had made a fake bank statement when applying for a U.S. student visa. After their first meeting in the International Student Office on campus, they drowned their sorrows from time to time with coffee in the school cafeteria, since it was the only thing they could both afford. David, he thought, might help him find a way out of his dire financial straits.

He called David and invited him to his apartment to talk about financial hardships and finding a job over a morning cup of tea. He arrived at the apartment dressed in khaki combat pants with bulging pockets and a black shirt.

"Come on in," Deepak pointed towards the chair by the sofa.

"We are both in the same situation, man, the same boat," David repeated what he had mentioned on the phone as he sat down. He looked tired. "I am broke," he continued, raising his fist in a fit of fury. "I bought a car by borrowing some money from my friend because I thought I needed it when I got a job. It turns out, finding a job is harder than it sounds and I had to sell the

127

car again to pay my friend's money back. Now, I don't have a car or a job; I'm at a loss."

"What can we do, David?" Deepak said. "I don't know any alternate way to earn money. At least, at the bagel store, I was working and getting paid. This life sucks man." Deepak entered the kitchen, saying "let me make some tea."

"Let's do something," David jumped out of the chair as if bitten by a bug. He seemed to think frantically, then burst out with, "Let's make balloon animals!"

"What is that, balloon animals?" Deepak asked, lifting his eyebrows while taking out a saucepan for making tea. He filled that with some water from the tap and put on the stove. He had never heard of balloon animals; he thought that perhaps David had lost his mind.

"It's a good idea, man. I'll teach you how to make them; it's easy. We can sell them to customers in restaurants so we can earn some tips. What do you think?" David smiled, sitting back in the chair. Deepak thought that it was the smile of pain.

"Not a bad idea," Deepak said. "But where is there a restaurant near here? How can we get to it? We don't have a car."

"Shit, that's gonna be another problem," David's expression fell. "That's true."

"Are there any restaurants nearby, so we don't have to drive?"

"I don't think so," David said. "I hate America now, man. Without a car, we can't do anything." David thought for a while. The steady hum of the refrigerator and the air- conditioning and the boiling tea were the only noises to be heard. He got up and felt weary again. "Hey, man, you know, I'm tired, Deepak. I'm not gonna stay here anymore. I'd rather go back to my country, for sure."

Deepak poured tea into two cups and tried to placate him, although he knew exactly how he felt.

"Don't say that, my friend, chill out. Try to struggle. This is the land of opportunity. One day, we will find our destinies. Don't lose your patience." He brought them and handed one cup to David. "I know, David, I'm in the same situation, remember?"

"Oh, I know!" David said immediately, without paying much attention to what Deepak said, holding a cup of tea. "Thank you for the tea, man."

"What?"

"There is one restaurant nearby, but we have to walk about two hours. Can we do that?"

"Why not—if we can make money, David? That's awesome!" Deepak exclaimed. "By the way I also know about other restaurants. They are just a mile away from here. You know Sunny Bagel where I worked, yes, that's the place where I have seen many restaurants around."

"Really, that's great bro," David said, drinking a sip of hot tea in excitement even without realizing how hot it was. "Fuck, it was fucking hot man, it fucking burned my tongue."

Deepak laughed out loud at him spitting out the hot tea right in front of him that sputtered all over him and the carpet.

"I am sorry bro," Deepak said laughing. "You should have known that it was hot, man. "Look at the tea is still steaming."

Finally, they made a plan. They agreed to sell balloon animals to the customers in a restaurant.

* * *

The next day, they pooled the last money they had to buy balloons. Although Deepak helped, David blew up most of the balloons. His face, especially his cheeks, turned bright red every time he blew into the colorful assortment of balloons. He taught Deepak how to make balloon animals, twisting and forming the balloons into a variety of shapes that resembled animals. They both started going to an Italian restaurant on weekends and the owners allowed them to sell their balloon creations. Each weekend, they walked a mile to get to the restaurant. On a good weekend, they earned about $200.

It was the first week of January. They wrapped themselves up with jackets, gloves, and scarfs and headed toward the restaurants without noticing how cold the weather was outside. The temperature at times fell below zero and sometimes cold air and blizzards blew their scarf away. They walked and ran covering themselves up as much as possible, hugging themselves and warding off the severe cold weather.

"I never imagined that I would struggle this way in the US, my friend," Deepak told David on their way to work.

"Me neither," he shouted as it was slightly windy and snowing thinly.

"I must write a novel about my struggle here."

"Put my name in your novel," David joked and laughed boisterously.

"Sure, man, I will," Deepak joined in the laughter. "You will be the protagonist in my novel. How about that?" They both laughed.

Winter in Georgia was odd, sometimes sunny, and at other times, frost lay on the ground and carpeted the grass, creating mulch in crystal ice patterns. It rained often, causing the temperature to drop drastically and the air to become frosty.

"If you becoming an author and me being a protagonist will earn some real money, sign me up," David said, hugging himself and walking.

Walking the long distance made them tired, but not sweaty. They cherished these light moments.

They together continued selling balloon animals for two weeks, that helped them collect around $1500 each. That was, at least, enough to pay the spring semester tuition fee for Deepak but he would need more for rent and food, but he could not continue to work in such severe cold weather. After that, Deepak left to accompany David.

"I am fucking going to die, man in such weather. I cannot work like this anymore," Deepak said. It was his third time he used the word "fuck." David continued to sell balloon animals on his own. The classes of spring semester would start the next day. Deepak thought of Melissa whom he had not seen and talked to for more than a month.

Chapter 19: Surprises

It was the first day of the second semester. Around 8 A.M., Deepak got a telephone call from Carole, the advisor of the International Students Admission Office, to tell him to see her. Deepak became nervous wondering about what could be the reason. *Did people discover him working off campus and she wanted to discuss that? If they find me out that, won't they deport me back to Nepal? How about my American dream?*

With these questions in mind, he went to the college to meet with Carole. He knocked on the door and Carole invited him in with a smile on her face, that comforted him and confided in him that it was not what he was skeptical of. Her face belied Deepak's doubt. He looked around her office— two computers on her table side by side, her and her family's pictures in a square frame on the table and her certificate against the wall, a book case in the corner, and two chairs in front of her.

"Oh, Deepak come on in," she invited him to sit in the chair she pointed.

Thanking her, he sat in a chair.

Her office was decorated with at least fifty falcons. Some were tiny; others seemed like she had visited a taxidermist and bought spare falcons at a bargain price. Carole was a true supporter of the university and its mascot. Her desk was covered with paper; there did not seem to be any order, but she somehow knew where everything was.

"We have good news for you. Considering your financial hardships and good GPA in class, we have decided to offer you some scholarship that goes toward your tuition fee so this semester you will pay only a thousand dollars. If you fail to keep your GPA high, you will lose this scholarship," she said.

Deepak was at a loss for words. He had no clue how to thank her for what he heard from her. He had not even thought about that. It dawned on him that America is the land of opportunity and it is a dreamland. He wanted to hug her and cry in joy. Fortunes come in a row when it starts, Deepak realized.

"Thank you, thank you very much," Deepak just said that for not finding the right words how to thank her. Tears of joy just rolled down by themselves. Carole saw them.

"You will be fine, Deepak. You have miles to go. As I said you have to maintain a 3.5 GPA every semester. I'm happy for you, Deepak," Carole beamed.

"Sure," Deepak smiled. "I will work hard." He thanked her again.

"I understand your situation, but don't worry, things will get better," Carole smiled again before he left her office. He left Carole's office.

He sat on a bench on campus, looking around: college students passed by him, locked in their own conversations. A boyfriend kissed his girlfriend, drawing his attention to them. Now these American kisses were not new to him. Wherever he went kisses did not leave him. Vanessa appeared and again disappeared from his memory. *When I meet Melissa, I will tell her my good news,* Deepak thought silently.

He walked to the library. In the library, he took a free copy of *The New York Times* from the newsstand, walked out, and sat on a swing, reading the newspaper and watching the scene on campus. It was green, and the flowers were blooming pink, yellow, and red. His imagination started to run away with him. *I want to graduate soon, get a job, buy a nice car, buy a big house, marry Melissa, and start living in the U.S. and won't go back home, invite my parents over here.*

Back at home, people fought about race, caste, ethnicity, language, religion, institution, and geography. Strikes made life a mess, as people were stranded when transportation stopped. "We want our separate state," one group shouted. Another other group screamed, "We need Madesh Pradesh. If we are refused, we won't hesitate to split heads open." Houses were burned down. Tear gas pervaded the streets and city. People scrambled, ran to save their lives.

"What's up, dude?" Ganesh's voice scared Deepak, breaking into his daydream. "Are you alright?" Ganesh had spotted Deepak staring vacantly.

"Yes, I'm alright," Deepak said, quickly coming to his senses. "I got a tuition scholarship brother."

"Oh, that's good. Congrats, bro" he gave a fist bump. "I gotta run for another class. Good to see you. I'll catch you later." Ganesh left.

It was also time for Deepak's Advanced poetry class, so he gathered his things together, stuffed the newspaper into his backpack, and walked the few blocks to the English building. Melissa was already there, and she smiled at him as he entered the classroom.

"Wow, great to see you, Melissa" Deepak said in a jovial mood. "How was your Christmas? How is your family?" Like previous days, he sat next to her and whispered into her ears. "I missed you."

"I missed you too," she said slowly.

"We will talk after class," Deepak said. "I have good news for you." All the students in class were looking at the professor's PowerPoint on the projector. She gave an overview of the semester and introduced them to different assignments the students would turn in.

After the class, the same normal routine followed.

"You were saying 'good news' earlier," Melissa said. "What's that?"

"Oh, I got a tuition scholarship. Now I have to pay only a thousand dollars per semester."

134

"Wow, that's great, Deepak. I am so happy for you."

They both got in the car.

"Did you miss me?" Melissa said. "But you never called me."

"Of course, I missed you. I thought you were with you family so I wanted you to spend time with your family. You also could have called me."

"I am sorry. I didn't know whether you were at work or home. I should have sent you a message. My bad. But I missed you," she said and reached to the back of the car and handed him a bag. "This is my gift from Texas. Open it." Deepak opened it and found a t-shit with a logo in the front that said Arlington, Texas where Melissa had come from.

"Wow, thank you so much" Deepak said and hugged her and kissed on the side of her neck. "It looks so nice."

"My pleasure," she said and drove the car.

She dropped him off like other days.

"Hey, let's go to the Star-Bucks coffee shop sometime and read our poems over a coffee drink when you have free time," she said and hugged him saying "goodbye."

"Sure, that sounds like a plan. I am excited. I will let you know," Deepak said. They exchanged a warm look with an anticipation of meeting soon.

As Deepak entered the apartment, his phone rang. "Unknown caller" appeared on the phone screen. He pressed the button to answer.

"Hello," Deepak answered. "Deepak, this is your father."

"How are you, *buwa*, how is everything?"

"Not very well." His father's voice sounded weak and strained.

"Why? What happened?" Deepak hesitated, fear crawling over him.

"Your mother is very sick and I need some money for her treatment. I don't want to ask you, but we need at least 200,000 Nepali rupees for her operation." That was around 1,500 American dollars, Deepak configured quickly.

Deepak swallowed hard and his hand gripped the phone tighter as he attempted to steady himself.

"Don't worry! I will manage it." Deepak found himself immediately saying aloud after he hung up the phone. "Where the hell am I going to find that money?" He mumbled.

He looked around as if the money would suddenly appear magically. His mind raced, his stomach began churning and he ran to the bathroom and vomited. Back in his bedroom, he examined the contents of his wallet. "Not much, how will I pay the rent, plus tuition fees, plus send money to help my mother? What he had was $1500 he made from the balloon animals business. *Shit! Shit! I can barely support myself, and now this! God, why do you hate me? All I wanted was to be happy, to make a little money, to be successful. Is that a crime?* He continued mumbling.

He glanced at his watch and saw that it was already 8 p.m. He realized he could collect his wages from the bagel store. After they had fired him, he had never been back. They owed him money; it's not much, but could help. It was a long shot, but perhaps he could ask Vikas to lend him some money. The bagel store would close at 10 p.m., so he would have to hurry. The bus hours were only until 7 P.M. He could have asked Melisssa for a favor but didn't want to bother her. He grabbed his jacket, put a scarf around, and ran. He ran most of the two miles to the bagel store. It was freezing, but his running and stress didn't let him feel that. He arrived panting. Vikas was still there trying to close the store. Surprised at seeing him, Vikas met the out-of-breath Deepak with a quizzical stare.

"Deepak, why are you here? Is everything okay?" He gave Deepak his full attention, knowing that something was very wrong. Deepak fought to find breath in his tight chest. His legs buckled beneath him and he steadied them with will- power. His tongue stuck to the roof of his mouth and refused to form words properly. "May I drink this water?" He drank tap water from a cup. Perspiration trickled into his mouth making the water salty.

"Vikas, my mom is very sick back home. She needs to get an operation. My father does not have money. I seriously need some money. Is there any way you can help me? I will pay you back," Deepak said in his trembling voice.

"I can give you only the money we owe you. I don't have more than that," Vikas said, as if he has other important things to listen.

"I beg you. I will come to work for nothing, I will pay you back. Please help me," Deepak clasped his hands in front of him and bowed his head.

"I'm sorry. I can't do that! Just take this money that I need to pay you," Vikas spoke without emotion and handed him $300 in cash from the register. *Fucking money-minded people, no heart of these people. Capitalism sucks. People have forgotten about humanity in this country.* He swore using the word "fuck" a fourth time.

Deepak grabbed the money, put it in his backpack and left. "Not enough, but at least this will help my father to begin the treatment," he whispered. It was already 11 p.m., there was no bus and it would take more than an hour to reach the apartment. He thought to stop by Wal-Mart and send the money through the Western Union money transfer system. Wal-Mart was around a mile and a half away from the bagel store. He picked up his pace. With each step, his backpack stuck to his back and increased in weight. The roads were almost deserted. A few cars passed him as he struggled toward his goal. It started drizzling and the light rain refreshed his face.

He had walked this route many times before, but today it seemed to go on and on. Streetlights were few and far between and the headlights of cars illuminated the road for only a second as they passed. Deepak felt uneasy, but he had to make it to Wal-Mart. He began to run the more he thought about his mother. He darted across the road and ran with what little energy he had left. He did not know when he got there, but he finally found himself in Wal-Mart. His hands trembled as he filled out the forms in quiet desperation.

His money that he made from balloon animals and the money from the bagel store made a total of $1800. The money was sent, and he was alive.

He made it back to the apartment. In the quiet of his apartment, Deepak began to breathe again. It was done. He didn't want to think of anything ahead. He just cherished the satisfaction he received from sending the amount of $1800 to his parents for the first time since he came to the USA despite his financial hardships. Joy could be in pain, he realized.

Chapter 20: Comings and goings

Deepak had stopped going to sell balloon animals. One month of the spring semester had passed. He still didn't have a job. He had borrowed another thousand dollars from his same friend in New Hampshire and paid the tuition fee. It was the month of February. The weather was still chilly. He had only two more semesters to go, and leaving now would mean defeat. If America had taught him anything, it was that he was not a man that was going to be easily defeated.

The phone rang. Deepak had just finished his lunch and was typing on his laptop in his own living room, working on his assignments for his evening classes.

"Hello?"

"How're you doing, Deepak? This is Vikas."

"I'm good," he said calmly, trying to tame his excitement, hoping he would offer his job back. "How are you?"

"Good, good," he sniffed. "I have a question."

"What's that?"

"Do you want to work? If you do, I want you to continue working only at Succulent Sandwiches, but not at the bagel store." Vikas realized that Deepak needed work. He was not as heartless as he seemed. Deepak's attempts to beg for money to help his mother must have touched his heart. Furthermore, he knew that a person in need of money would work hard, and Vikas needed a hardworking person.

"Sure, Vikas, I will."

"Then, come tomorrow at Succulent Sandwiches at 10 in the morning," he said. "You can work three days a week for now."

"Thank you, Vikas, very much."

Deepak hung up the phone and gave a deep sigh.

He walked into the kitchen, got some water from the tap and drank.

Working at Succulent Sandwiches, he could get less money than he would selling animal balloons, but he couldn't tolerate the cold weather and walking a long distance on foot. Now Deepak didn't need that much money since he was given a tuition scholarship. He just needed a few more bucks to pay rent and for food until he would graduate and find a job to pay the loan back home and his friend's money in New Hampshire.

Suddenly, Lucas—who had practically been a stranger in the apartment—came in quickly through the door. He looked stressed and tense as he tossed his backpack by the kitchen and made some food.

"Deepak, I need to talk to you," Lucas said.

Deepak shuddered in foreboding at what he might say. He wondered if he had made a mistake or something.

"Of course, Lucas, where have you been last a few days?" Deepak said

"Oh, at my friend's house," Lucas said. "Sorry, I should have let you know about that." He continued. "I am moving out of this. If you don't have someone to go live with, you can find a roommate and stay here. The lease is due to expire, and I'm not going to renew it. You still have one more week, so you don't have to rush."

"Only one week," Deepak muttered. He had no idea what he was going to do. Every time he solved one problem, another seemed to come up. He couldn't rent an apartment on his own because he did not have a social security number or enough money. The only people that might be able to help him were probably David or Ganesh.

"Are you really leaving, Lucas?" Deepak asked, his voice straining.

"Yeah," Lucas said, then added, almost apologetically, "Sorry, man."

Deepak looked outside the window. He saw bare trees. He grabbed his backpack and left for the college to take his evening classes. He was glad that he was going to see Melissa in class. As soon as he reached the college and his classroom, he saw Melissa standing by the classroom like the others, waiting for the professor to arrive. As soon as she saw Deepak, she smiled at him.

"How are you?" Melissa said, her pretty eyes winking. "Want to go grab a coffee very quick?"

"I am fine! How are you?" Deepak responded. "Oh, yes, sure!" They headed towards the cafeteria quickly and purchased two cups of coffee. Melissa paid, and they headed back to the classroom.

Immediately, the professor entered the classroom and everybody followed him. Melissa sat next to Deepak making him feel her intimate presence. Melissa touched his hands under the desk and smiled looking into his eyes, gesturing to wait after class. Deepak dropped his eyelids accepting her proposal. They enjoyed the class together over sips of coffee. After class, the routine followed.

Chapter 21: Back at Succulent Sandwiches

The next morning, Deepak stood in the doorway of Succulent Sandwiches, where Rita was opening the store. When she saw him, she smiled, and he beamed back. She looked enthusiastic, energetic, and high-spirited. After last night's conversation with Lucas, Deepak's spirit was very low. He was wondering whether he could find another room or a roommate within a week so he could move out of the apartment he was living in. Still, he was relieved to be working again.

Rita asked him why he had been absent for so long. Deepak explained everything to her.

"Why didn't you tell me?" Rita said. "I could come to your apartment to see you. I could bring you some meal."

"No, I was okay, again thought you were perhaps busy," Deepak defended.

"When you are sick, you should let me know. That is what it means to be us in a foreign country, to help each other, you know?"

"Sure, *didi*," Deepak said, putting the gloves in his hand, becoming ready for making sandwiches.

He had known how to do everything in Succulent Sandwiches from sweeping and mopping the floor to washing dishes and making sandwiches.

However, the glow of coming back to work faded fast. Two-dozen dishes were left in the sink, and he started to wash them first.

"Deepak, *bhai*, this is not the way to wash the dishes. Look here," Rita said, pulling the dishes from his hand. She showed him how to pre-wash the dishes and then use the dishwasher, putting them in their proper places. After they were cleaned, she wanted him to separate the lids from the bowls.

"Alright, alright, I will do it," Deepak said

"Don't be hasty. Listen to me closely. Look at what I'm doing here," she said in a domineering voice. *Is she trying to be bossy to me?* Deepak asked himself silently. *Maybe she is not trying to be bossy. Maybe she is generous by nature and she is teaching me how to do things very well.* He consoled himself. Still, her attitude bothered him. Deepak w a s too sensitive, but he tried to stay silent.

"This is a very good job you have," she said. "Compared to when I used to work at the restaurant, these dishes you're washing are nothing. I had much, much more to do."

"How could washing dishes be a very good job?" Deepak wanted to ask her. Rather than voicing his complaints, Deepak just nodded his head in approval. He realized she must have suffered more than he suffered. He appreciated that she came from a different place, but the weight of being looked down on by someone still felt heavy in his heart.

"You're also lucky to get a job since it's illegal for you to work," she said, placing a tip-box next to the register. "How much are you paid?"

"Five dollars per hour," Deepak said.

"Bhai, that's not bad," she said. "I started from $5 even though I was a green card holder, and the manager never paid me on time. Now, I'm paid $10 per hour, and Vikas treats us well, too." As she spoke, she put a dollar bill from the register into the tip jar.

"Why are you putting the money in the tip jar?" Deepak looking puzzled.

She shook her head and smiled knowingly. "Don't you know money attracts money? If I put money in there, customers might give more tips. At the end of the day, I will put the dollar bill back into the register."

"The work I am doing has nothing to do with my

English major back in Nepal," Deepak tried to change the subject of discussion.

"Everyone washes dishes in America, no matter what his education back in Nepal was," she said. "I earn more than a minister in Nepal earns. I don't care what kind of job I am doing." She was back to her usual diatribe. She started counting the money at the register, not missing even a penny of the cash in the opening.

"Yes, you really do earn very good money," Deepak said biting his tongue.

"The only thing I miss is all my relatives back home," she said. "Every year, I miss the festival and reunions with my relatives."

"When will you go back home?" Deepak asked out of politeness.

"I'm not sure because my daughter is studying here. I'm doing all this for the future of my daughter. I need to stay until she is able to stand on her own two feet," she said putting the bread loaves into the oven.

"I know," Deepak said. At the same time, her phone rang, and she went to the back, saying, "Watch the bread in the oven. Don't let it burn." Deepak took the customer's order and did some busy work around the cashier. Half an hour later, Rita appeared phone in hand.

"I hate talking on the phone for a long time," she said.

"Then why were you talking on the phone so long?" Deepak wanted to ask her, but he just snickered at her foolishness.

Deepak silently adored a few things about her. She was a hard worker. When she worked, she put her heart into it. She knew everything at Succulent Sandwiches that she had to do. She kept the store neat and clean and in perfect working order. One could tell that from looking at her scrubbing or sweeping or cleaning all the time even while talking.

144

"Can you fill up the ice?" she asked Deepak.

"Okay," Deepak said. He reached to grab a bucket by the ice machine and started pouring ice into the bucket and then in the big box by the register.

"What happened?" she asked Deepak. "You look like you're about to cry."

"I don't know. Maybe some dust entered my eyes," Deepak tried to deflect the question, wiping his eyes with the back of his palm. In truth, there was no dust; the pain of having to struggle every minute of the day without his family around in a foreign land was weighing him down again. She knew the pain because she had also gone through the same situation.

"Give me the bucket, and I'll fill the rest," she said, grabbing the bucket from Deepak's hand. "You just rest a little bit before it gets busy," she continued, "At least you have a future. I have nothing else to do. Whatever I do is for my daughter." She filled the ice as Deepak started sweeping the floor.

In the evening, Vikas came to the store and counted off some money to give Deepak his pay. The rent was due and Deepak needed to keep a roof over his head.

He thought he would call Melissa to pick him up and stop by the coffee house on the way and chat with Melissa over a cup of coffee.

Melissa came right away to pick him up. They drove to the Star Bucks coffee house on the way. Parked the car. Entered the coffee place. Melissa took out money to pay for it.

"No, no Melissa, I will pay for it. I am paid today," Deepak pushed her money away and gave a 20 dollar bill to the cashier.

The sat outside around a table under an umbrella. It was 5 P.M.

"Do you have poems to read?" Melissa asked over a sip of coffee. Deepak always had a piece of

145

paper or two scribbled with some kind of poems, mostly about Melissa.

"Yes, I do," he said. "May I read?"

"Oh please."

Taking a piece of paper from his wallet, Deepak started reading.

The ocean is blue
As blue as your eyes
And the size of your eyes lures me
The dancing hair and the shaking lips
Is in tune with the beating of my heart,
Filling me with passion;
Can I embrace you
And shower you with affection
Without hurting you?

He watched how her hair danced as he read the poem. Her lips flew with emotions and feelings and her cheeks glowed. Melissa clapped, saying "wow, so beautiful" and took another coffee sip.

"Now your turn," Deepak said, holding his coffee cup and sipping it.

"Mine is not as beautiful as yours," she said.

"You are more beautiful than the poem that will come to your poetry so no worries,"

"Aw, very sweet of you. Thank you" she said, taking a piece of paper from her purse. She read.

If I were you,
I would go ahead full of confidence
Without shyness
As the chariot of his royal highness moves forward,
And grab your hand and kiss it,
Kneeling down in front of you,
To pay homage for you in love,
But I am a woman
So you should do that for me,
Though I can, I cannot.

146

Melissa dropped Deepak off at the apartment, gave him a big tight hug.

"It was a beautiful poem, thank you," she whispered into his ears.

"Yours too," he said. "Good night. Sleep well."

Lucas was at home. He handed all the money he had earned to Lucas, who took it with barely a grunt of gratitude.

He was exhausted. He lay down on the sofa. "My feet burned," he whispered. He wished more than anything for the light touch of his mother's fingers as she kneaded mustard oil into his tired limbs while in Nepal.

In his imagination, Vanessa followed by Melissa appeared out of nowhere. She glided into the room and slowly came to his bed with a bowl of sweetly perfumed essential oil in her hand. She sat by Deepak, pulled his legs into her lap, and started massaging his feet, smiling all the while. When she finished, she hugged him, kissed him and left.

Actually, Vanessa was not there, nor Melissa. Deepak was alone in the apartment. Vanessa still hadn't returned since her dispute with Lucas. He knew he had to find someone to live with. He phoned Ganesh that night.

"Hello, Ganesh, this is Deepak. How're you doing?" "I'm alright. You?"

"Good, brother. What do you think about living together as roommates?" Deepak asked. He then explained the situation between Vanessa and Lucas.

"I was thinking of moving to a different place closer to the university, or living in a dorm, but wasn't sure who I could live with."

Ganesh confided in Deepak and told him that he was currently living with a family, but the place was not really conducive for studying.

"Then let's stay together," Deepak told him. "We are, in one way or another, brothers."

147

"It's not a big deal. Let me think. I'm going to bed now.

Talk to you tomorrow, Deepak. Give me a call."

"Alright," Deepak said, and hung up the phone, hoping for the best.

Chapter 22: Poetry in Motion

Time passed. Two semesters were over. The fall started. The winter was gone. The trees had started coming back to their lives, and Squirrels started marching here and there, up and below. Deepak concluded he never liked winter.

When Deepak started spending time with Melissa, even months and semester just flew by. In the beginning days, even a single day felt like a month to Deepak, but now a day felt like a second.

He and Melissa started spending more times outside than on campus or in class, mostly at coffee shops, reading each other's poetry, almost every day, especially in the evening when Deepak had to go to Succulent Sandwiches during the day.

Deepak was getting ready for going out with Melissa as they had planned to go out to watch a movie in the theater hall. He had asked Vikas to give him time off for a different reason. He was waiting for Melissa to come and pick him up. He was thinking of holding her hands while watching the movie and conveying his thoughts and emotions in any meaningful way.

He glanced at his phone and recognized Vikas' number calling him. Today was his day off. Deepak didn't want to answer his phone, but Vikas was paying him, so he answered reluctantly.

"Hello?" Deepak said.

"Deepak, I need your help," Vikas sniffed.

"What kind of help, Vikas?"

"I need you to come to Succulent Sandwiches and help me work for three hours."

"I have not done my assignment for the class tonight, Vikas," Deepak lied. He didn't want to tell him that he was planning to go watch a movie with Melissa. He knew his plea would fall on deaf ears, for Vikas' business was more important to him than Deepak's education.

"I need your help right now, please," he said.

Deepak didn't want to get fired a second time, so he finally agreed. "I'll be there soon," Deepak said. He called Melissa and let her know about the situation before she would come and pick him up. "When I am done with the work, I will call you," he said. "I am sorry"

"No worries, dear, I understand," she said.

Deepak threw on his uniform and prayed he would find time to write a poem for the class. Rita was on leave, so Deepak worked with Vikas. Working with the manager was stressful, and he felt as though he was always being watched. He washed dishes, swept the floor, and made sandwiches for customers. Vikas seemed happy with Deepak's work, but did not give him even a short rest, which meant he had no time to write his poem at work.

After three hours of work, Vikas gave him him off.

"You can go home, now if you have class today and do the assignments as you were saying." Vikas said.

Deepak left Succulent Sandwiches and called Melissa to pick him up. She drove to the mall where he was waiting outside.

"Are you going to watch a movie today?" she asked.

"Are we?" Deepak questioned. "I am in the work uniform and it stinks. If you don't mind let's watch some other time. What do you think?"

"Sure" Melissa said. "How about stopping by the coffee shop, chatting, and reading our poems over coffee sips if you want?"

"Sounds good to me."

Melissa drove the car and parked outside the coffee shop. Like other regular days, they grabbed coffee, sat around the table, took the pieces of paper and became ready to read the poems they had scribbled.

"You start first," Melissa proposed.

"Fine," Deepak said and unfolded the piece of paper. "Okay, now I start." Both coffee cups were right in front of them face to face.

What a feeling!
It spills over my body and sways me away
What a feeling!
Tasteless Odorless Colorless
Just amorphous
And again I wince once for the cause of it.
It wets me down like a downpour does.
What a feeling!
Tender, Fragile
Melts like a wax, Burns like a wick.
And kills me,
Kills me with kindness
What a feeling!

Melissa seemed very pleased with his poem. It hit her that she liked him. She moved her chair, came closer to Deepak, and sat next to him. She held his hands and said in a voice that was filled with a lot of emotions "I really liked your poem. The feelings are amazing."

"Thank you," Deepak massaged her hands with a look of love into her eyes. "Now your turn."

"Okay," she took a deep breath and smiled looking at Deepak, unfolded her piece of paper and started reading.

Love is the stuff that dreams are made of
Concrete, hard, holds you firm
When you feel you are slipping
Away from the reality of things,
It is granite, it welds and forms
Something out of nothing, like
The way you helped me focus
My mind and created
Order out of chaos
These words are penned for you
Although they are not read
They are written for you
And you understand them

151

"Wow, beautiful," Deepak said. "Indeed, love is the stuff that dreams are made of."

They grabbed the coffee on the table and sipped it.

"You look amazing, Melissa," Deepak said.

She was dressed in her favorite blue color outfit and her hair was braided on both sides. Deepak went closer, close enough for his eyes to touch her eyes, almost ready to kiss each other. They heard the breathing and felt its warmth. Before their lips met, Melissa just pushed herself back and said "you know I have something here we can take a bite of with this coffee."

She reached into her bag and pulled out two small bars of chocolate. She handed one to Deepak. As he reached to take it, their fingers touched briefly, and she withdrew her hand as if it had been burned. Deepak thought she really liked him too. He thanked her for the chocolate. He didn't like sweet things, but all the sweets from her were the only sweets he would like.

They left. Melissa drove him to his apartment. The routine followed.

Chapter 23: friends and enemies

True to his word, Lucas had already left the apartment. Ganesh and Deepak had started living in a different apartment. The third semester was going to be over soon. It had already been more than a year since Deepak came to the US.

It was a two bedroom apartment in the same complex where Deepak lived sharing the living room with Lucas and Vanessa. The apartment was more spacious and he had his own private space, way better than his first place.

Things between Ganesh and Deepak were not going straight after a couple of months of their stay in the apartment. It was not about the quarrel or any argument between the two, but because of the uncomfortable feelings due to Ganesh's attitudes.

One day, while studying in his new apartment, Deepak turned around and saw that Ganesh was listening to Nepali deusi songs online, probably trying to imagine the ambiance of the *Tihar* festival that would be celebrated thousands of miles away in Nepal every year. Never before had Deepak heard him listening to *deusi* songs, just English rap music. This was the second Tihar Deepak was missing after he came to the US.

"This was a song we used to sing during deusi," Ganesh said, staring at Deepak wistfully, almost begging Deepak to listen and share the joyous moment with him. As Deepak listened with him, he realized that one's roots and culture were, indeed, powerful elements; no matter how long a person lived on foreign shores.

Ganesh had missed *Dashain* and *Tihar* and a list of other Nepali festivals every year for the past five years.

"Whenever *Tihar* arrives, I can't help but cry,"

Deepak croaked painfully. "It breaks my heart to think of my sister including *dhaka topi* and marigold garlands on her festival shopping list when *bhai tika* arrives each year. I'm alone here, with nothing but sweet memories of the festival I celebrated with my family back home." When Deepak breathed in, he seemed to inhale the imaginary aroma of the freshly cooked sel rotis that were made during *Tihar.*

"I remembered my sister whom I have not seen for a long time," Ganesh said looking at the laptop's screen. Deepak realized Ganesh was not that stupid. He was also an emotional person and could not forget his past, culture, and festival although he seemed to be acting differently in those previous days with Deepak.

Ganesh recalled the candle-lit households and sounds of firecrackers. He remembered having fun playing cards with his friends and relatives and playing *deusi* around the neighborhood. Overcome with fond memories, he suddenly became teary-eyed as well.

"My friend, you're not the only one who gets homesick during the festivals. The reality is, most of the Nepalese living abroad feel the same. Though it is a matter of pride to have made it to the US, it can also be painful at times," Deepak said while sitting in the same chair and facing toward him. Deepak found himself in Ganesh's nostalgia.

After a while, Deepak left for campus early to get some fresh air. As he walked on the central pathway to the English building, he saw a familiar face in the distance. It was Lucas. Deepak greeted him but did not ask about or for Vanessa. He entered the class where Melissa was already in.

After class, Deepak rushed home without waiting for Melissa as he had to drop a letter at the mailbox of the post office so he thought he would ask Ganesh for a favor. Deepak texted Melissa and said he had to go.

"Ganesh, can you give me a ride to the post

office, I have to mail a letter?" Deepak asked him for a favor as soon as he entered the apartment. Ganesh was busy doing something in his laptop.

"Let's go tomorrow," he said, turning in his swivel chair like a cameraman, panning left and right. "I have to respond to my emails."

Deepak missed Vanessa, her smile, the soft Spanish lilt in her voice. Deepak missed the journeys in her car to the supermarket. Every time Deepak had to go to some place, Vanessa was always there. Now, he had to wait on Ganesh. But Ganesh was far from being reliable.

"Can you respond to them later?" Deepak asked.

"You're not the only one who has work to do. Why can't you wait until tomorrow?" Ganesh scowled, but finally gave in and threw up his hands. "Okay, okay, let's go. You're impatient, man."

They got into the car and headed toward the post office. "You need to be patient," Ganesh reminded him, stopping the car at the stop sign.

Trying to change the subject, Deepak asked, "Why did you stop the car?"

"Are you blind? Don't you see the stop sign?" he said. Deepak kept silent. "If I violate the traffic rules, will you pay for the ticket?"

"Don't worry, man. It's not a big deal," Deepak mimicked his friend, jokingly.

"Fuck you," Ganesh said shortly.

"What?" Deepak asked. Deepak also had started swearing, but had never sworn on someone in face. It hurt him. He really didn't like how Ganesh spoke to him. Even if he thought Ganesh was a nice guy, spoken words mattered.

"I have helped many friends, but they forget about me later," he said. "Bullshit."

How can they remember such a jerk? Deepak said silently so only he could hear. *You don't even know how to respect your friends.*

"Don't worry. They will remember your selfless help and charming attitude," Deepak said sarcastically, but then added sincerely, "You've helped me a lot, brother. If you weren't there, I would not have a job."

"You were lucky to get a job so quickly at Succulent Sandwiches and the bagel store, you know?" he reminded.

"I don't know if I could call washing dishes lucky. But I suppose."

"Who are you? You're nothing. There are many people who are more educated than you and work such jobs. I've been living here for many years and am still working at a gas station. You didn't struggle as much as I struggled," he snapped back angrily. What Ganesh said sounded more like what Rita had said.

You have not even graduated with your undergraduate degree, how would you be able to get a better job than working at a gas station? Deepak wanted to question him, but he kept silent.

"How long is it to the post office?" Deepak asked, changing the subject.

"This is why I tell you to be patient," Ganesh said. "You are boring sometimes."

"The poet John Berryman wrote, 'Life friend, is boring,' Deepak said smiling and teasing him.

"Have you ever written a poem?" Ganesh said.

"Of course. I am in the creative writing program, bro. I have an anthology of poems, ready to be published."

"There has to be good rhythm and music in a poem. Do you know that?" Ganesh tried to mentor him. *At least this man has some sense of some elements of a poem,* Deepak thought.

They reached the post office, and Deepak stayed in the line. There was a black lady standing akimbo next to Deepak. He instinctively spotted her exposed, protruding breasts.

156

"Don't look at them, or she will sue you," Ganesh warned him in Nepali so she would not understand.

They mailed the letter.

They returned home. On their way back home, Deepak did not speak to Ganesh anymore. As soon as they arrived, Ganesh went back to his swivel chair and started working on his laptop.

"Don't you get hungry?" Deepak asked Ganesh as he was busy in laptop.

"I have no time to cook, man."

"Let's make a schedule then," Deepak said. "I will cook on weekdays, and you cook on weekends."

"Let me think about it," Ganesh said. But Ganesh didn't even have enough time to cook on weekends.

He was too lazy even to cook for himself and would often satisfy his appetite by eating a sandwich. Sometimes he left the dishes in the sink to dry.

"I have brought my sandwich so I am fine with this. I do not need any dinner," he said sometimes.

If Deepak cooked Nepali food for him, he gobbled it all greedily.

"Can I finish the rest, brother?" Ganesh said when he saw the meal Deepak cooked in the kitchen.

Deepak also cooked food for himself and went to work at Succulent Sandwiches. When Deepak came back from work, it was late. He was exhausted and hungry. There was no food at all in the kitchen, and Ganesh, as usual, had not held up his end of the cooking schedule. Deepak boiled noodles and ate.

"Mom, if you were here, you would not let me be hungry," he wrote this in his diary. Deepak thought of his mother longingly.

This is how Deepak's third semester passed with Ganesh.

I should not have lived with Ganesh as a roommate, he whispered. *But he is a good guy. He found me a job.*

157

Still, Deepak could not tolerate Ganesh's attitude, and he had another option. David had called earlier and asked him if he was still looking for a place since he needed another person to share the rent.

Deepak decided to tell Ganesh he was moving out.

Towards the end of the November, Deepak decided to talk to Ganesh about it over breakfast.

"Ganesh, I need to leave the apartment," he said, bluntly. "I have found somewhere else to live."

"What the fuck?" he said. "Are you serious? We just leased it."

Ganesh's reaction further proved Deepak's point that he had to leave.

"I don't like the way you talk to me, Ganesh. I feel like you don't respect me," Deepak spoke his mind.

"The lease is in my name, and we have to pay two month's rent in advance if we're leaving," he said. "I came here for you, and you're pulling this shit. I am who I am, okay?"

"I know, Ganesh. You have done many wonderful things for me, and I will pay you back or find someone else to take my place. You found a job for me, and you have helped me a lot. I will never ever forget you, but I can't live with you."

With that, Deepak placed his month's rent on the table. He was carrying that money Vikas had paid just the other day.

"You are bullshit, man," Ganesh fumed, almost growling. "If I knew you would do this shit to me, I would have found my own way. I do good things for people, and everyone does bad things to me."

"That's not my intention, Ganesh," Deepak said softly.

"Shut your mouth," he said. "I don't need you, either. You can go wherever you'd like to go." Ganesh left the room, slamming the door behind.

In his heart, Deepak felt bad for Ganesh, but he knew staying there was toxic.

Chapter 24: Three Musketeers

Deepak woke up and looked outside the window. Trees started looking bare and naked. Leaves were falling off of the branches. Winter was about to enter. It was going to be the second winter. *Melissa is preparing to leave for her family in Texas to celebrate Christmas that was approaching. Oh, how fast, time flies,* Deepak thought. *Perhaps, after Melissa came into my life, I couldn't even feel the span of time.* He got up from the bed and left the house to see David who lived in another apartment in the same complex.

David opened the door and blinked in surprise when he saw Deepak on the other side. "Hey, how are you doing?" David said.

"Sorry to disturb you so early," Deepak said. "You weren't still asleep, were you?"

"It's okay. I was already up." David replied, though he still looked sleepy. "Come on in."

Deepak entered the room. David pointed him toward a chair to have a seat. "It's just a surprise, man. Why'd you come so early?" David asked.

Deepak looked around the room. The living room was very spacious. It was a one bedroom apartment. There was an AT&T router in the corner of the living room and nothing around besides a wooden chair and a desk. The bedroom door was ajar through which two lying mattresses with a crumpled bed cover appeared.

"I need a roommate," Deepak said. "Are you still looking for one?"

"Oh, yes!" David said, suddenly very awake. "I talked to my roommate and told him all about you the other day," he continued returning towards the bedroom door and calling someone. "Hee, c'mon in here and meet Deepak!"

160

Hee shuffled into the room, trying to clear the sleep from his eyes. Hee was so skinny that he looked like a scarecrow with clothes hanging off of him. His eyes were like shiny black pebbles caught in a crescent-moon and his wide smile seemed to stretch from ear to ear. He had large glasses that covered his face and wore a striped t-shirt that stuck to his skinny frame and black shorts that revealed boney knees.

"Hee, this is Deepak. He's from Nepal," David introduced him to Hee. "Deepak, this is my roommate, Hee."

"Nice to meet you," Hee said, shaking his hand. He smelled like a stale morning.

"Nice to meet you too," Deepak said.

"Deepak is looking for a roommate. What do you think about keeping him here?" David asked Hee.

"Oh, that's good then," Hee said.

"The more people we share the apartment with, the cheaper it is for each of us to pay rent," David explained. "Don't you think so? Okay let me make some coffee, guys. You two talk."

"Do you also work, Hee?" Deepak asked.

"Yes, yes," Hee said.

"Where?"

"What the hell? Restaurant!" he said. He seemed to use the phrase "what the hell?" with faux frustration every time someone asked him a question or if he had to explain something.

"How much do you earn?"

"What the hell! Not much," he said. "I only work weekends."

"What do you do there?"

"Waiter and dishwasher, what the hell!"

"How much are you paid?"

"What the hell! They do not pay. Tips. Tips... Sometimes $100 and sometimes $200."

"I also got a job at a gas station," David said.

"No more balloon animals for me."

"That's great," Deepak said and instantly felt much more at ease here. Hee was pacing here and there.

David made coffee in the kitchen and brought three cups. They chatted for a while over the sips.

They decided to move Deepak's stuff the same day.

They all went to Deepak's apartment. Ganesh was sitting in a chair in the living room, silent and quiet.

"Did you wake up bro," Deepak asked, trying to be a good friend of him. Ganesh acted like he did not hear what Deepak said. Deepak repeated himself one more time.

"Yes," Ganesh finally spoke. Deepak did not want to leave the apartment on a bad note.

"Now I am moving, brother" Deepak said pointing towards David and Hee. "They are here to help me move my stuff."

"Hi," both of them greeted Ganesh.

"That's good," Ganesh said without paying any attention. He remained quiet and unconcerned while they carried the boxes away. He acted as if he already forgotten Deepak, but Deepak did not want to end their relationship on a bad note.

* * *

Deepak, David, and Hee started living together sharing sorrows and happiness. They encroached three mattresses in one bedroom, one for each of them. All of them were international students. They started sharing each other's experiences from their countries to the USA, what it was like to be on a student visa in the USA. *Sharing pain helped mitigate peoples' collective agony,* Deepak realized.

Although they had different mother tongues, they could all understand homesickness and longing.

They had three different accents and, when two of them couldn't understand the other's accent, they would write what they meant to say down on paper. When they talked to their parents back home at the same time, the congestion of three different languages made the room fill with falling and rising tones and high and low intonations.

For the first time in a long time, Deepak felt he had a home away from home.

Chapter 25: Happiness and Romance

One month passed with David and Hee. Christmas was over. It was the month of January. Melissa was back from Texas celebrating Christmas with her family, a bit earlier than last time. That was what she had told Deepak over the phone, "I will be there a few days before the semester begins." Deepak also had enough time during Christmas to work more hours at Succulent Sandwiches and make some money to pay some tuition fee for the coming semester and pay rent and send some money back home.

His mother's operation back home was successful despite her sufferings from other chronic diseases like diabetes and high blood-pressure.

If you can cope with difficulties and hardships, the days after are always beautiful and promising, Deepak thought. He didn't have to worry much about the tuition fee; he had good friends to share the apartment; he had Melissa, his beautiful American girlfriend to hang out and share other things. *American dream is coming true,* he thought.

Deepak grabbed a laptop, thought of Vanessa. That was the laptop Vanessa had given him. He planned to register for the classes in the spring. Before he worked on it, he checked his Facebook page. It was the weekend and he had some time to relax and enjoy himself.

His roommates had already woken up and were making cereal breakfast for themselves. Deepak browsed his Facebook page as his roommates talked idly over oatmeal raisin cereal and milk. While he was going through his page, he saw Melissa had sent him a message. Warmth raced through his heart as he clicked on the message. It simply read: *Hi, Deepak! What are you up to today? If you're not doing anything, call me.* She also left her number on the bottom just in case.

Deepak could hear his friends leaving the apartment, calling out good-byes. He waited eagerly until they left, then called Melissa. Her voice sounded soft over the phone.

"Yes, Melissa," he said, "Are you back from Texas?"

"Oh, I'm glad you called. Oh yes. Remember I told you I would be here by now. What're your plans today?"

"Nothing. I'm off. Just...hanging out at home, thinking of you," Deepak said, and gave a little bit of extra talk with an intention of wooing her.

"Do you wanna play chess?" she said, her voice felt pleasant in Deepak's ear.

"Sure!" Deepak's face looked blushed and filled with excitement.

"Great! I'll come to pick you up and we can play chess at my place this afternoon."

"That sounds great," Deepak said, hoping his voice sounded calmer than he felt. "I'd love to see you."

She hung up and Deepak lingered with the phone by his ear, still hypnotized by her words. Her voice echoed around him, giving him a chilling sensation all across his body. He felt like he could dance with joy. He hummed and shook his head in a rhythmic motion of the song. Deepak made some lunch while listening to some Nepali music and after lunch, h e shaved his beard and took a shower. He tried to scrutinize himself in the mirror to see how he would look in front of Melissa.

In that moment, he forgot everything: Succulent Sandwiches o r his unrelenting money problems.

The phone rang. "Shit!" Deepak talked to himself. "I'm not ready yet." He grabbed the phone and, without looking at the number, said, "Hello, Melissa!"

"Ready?" she asked.

"Ready," Deepak said, quickly implementing a

couple last minute touch-ups. He didn't want to make her wait. He dressed himself up in a rush.

Before too long, she arrived at his apartment.

"Wow, you look handsome," she said when he opened the door.

"Thank you," Deepak said, beaming. "You're very pretty, too. Nice to see you after a month." She smiled back at him. Her smile surpassed the mystery of the Mona Lisa. Her beauty spellbound him from the day they first met. He tried to relax on the soft, comfortable leather seats inside her car. They found themselves stealing glances at each other as they traveled the few blocks to her home.

"How was the Christmas?" Deepak asked.

"Oh, it was awesome," she said, while driving. "Did you have a good time?"

"Yes, I did, but I missed you."

"Me too."

She parked her car right in front of her apartment in the parking lot.

This was the first time Deepak was inside her apartment. Her apartment was cozy, small and quaint. The floors were wood, and colorful rugs dotted the room. It was sparsely furnished: a cream loveseat and a couple of armchairs with low backs, decorated with velvet cushions. High-backed brown chairs adorned the simple lines of the tan and brown table that held a black and white chessboard set up, waiting for them to begin their game.

"It's very chilly," she said. "Would you like some tea or coffee?"

"That would be wonderful! Anything!" Deepak said. She checked the heating, and pointed toward a chair, offering him a seat. Her hospitality wooed Deepak even more. Deepak just sat in a chair and continued looking at Melissa making coffee. She brought two cups of coffee and some biscuits to the coffee table in front of Deepak.

166

They started playing chess over coffee and the snacks she brought over the table.

More than moving pawns, they conversed, smiled, and their fingers brushed. Deepak explained his struggle and frustration working at Succulent Sandwiches. She held both his hands and looked up at Deepak's eyes. "Your hard work will pay off. I know it."

"Thank you, Melissa." His eyes never left hers.

"I know that your religious background is Hindu, but what does that really mean?" she said, changing the topic, moving another pawn.

"I was born in a Hindu family, but as you know, I'm an open-minded person. I have been to the temple, church, and even monasteries." Deepak continued, "To me, all religions have many things in common: humanity, peace, brotherhood, and love."

She nodded.

"What about you? What does being Catholic mean to you?" Deepak asked moving a rook two steps down on the chess board.

"I am from an Irish Catholic family. We feel strongly about our religion. It's part of our identity," she said, giving Deepak a look of love.

"I know many people in America have kids before they marry, but in my culture, it is wrong to have sex before marriage." Deepak said even if he knew that he was treading in unchartered waters, but he needed for her to understand him better.

"I can't think of sex before marriage, either," she said. "After marriage, we're not supposed to divorce unless the husband beats up his wife. And those of us who do divorce, don't think of marrying a second time," she said.

"Oh really?" Deepak said, contemplating the Chess pawns and moving them and taking a mouthful of coffee. "That seems very similar to my thoughts on marriage."

167

From that point on, they spoke about politics and money. They didn't agree on much but remained respectful of each other's' position. They spoke about past loves, which made Deepak somewhat uncomfortable because he didn't want to think someone did or could want to ravage Melissa in the same way he did.

She must have sensed his longing and discomfort because she entwined her hand in his and pulled him closer, so close, he could feel her heartbeat. In all the time they had spent together, this was the first time that they had become physically close.

Deepak caressed her hair, pulling her head toward his and gently pulling her into a kiss. She kissed him back, and it filled up his soul. He breathed, "I love you, Melissa."

"I love you too," she sighed. He wanted to undress her, hold her on his lap and shower her with kisses, but he stopped himself, looking at his watch. It was already 9 P.M.

"It's getting late..." Deepak said. "I should go home. Otherwise, my roommate might wonder where I am."

"You can stay here if you want," she said showing the place. "You can sleep in my bed. I'll sleep on the couch." Deepak was tempted.

He felt in a Hamletian dilemma whether to stay there or to leave for his own apartment. *Love is fire that can sear so quickly*, Deepak realized.

"Okay, Melissa," I will just lie down on this couch here." Melissa brought a blanket. "Would you mind laying down here with me?"

"Sure, I can," she said and lay down on the couch next to Deepak, shoulder to shoulder. Fire had its own pace and its own root that slowly spread from kisses to the breasts and below. They started breathing heavily and "I love you" continuously conveyed their emotions, and finally they, without any intention of it, doused the fire of love. Deepak came outside and deeply kissed her.

"I am sorry," both of them exchanged because they had broken their promises that sex was not their thing before marriage that is what they had said in their conversation.

"I think I must go," Deepak said, fixing himself. "Otherwise my roommate might wonder where I had been for that too long."

"Alright," she said without further discussion. She dropped him off at his apartment, leaving him with a kiss that awakened desire, expectations, and longing one more time.

When Deepak reached the apartment, he found David lounging on the couch.

"Where've you been, man?" David asked. "I tried calling you."

"Sorry, I was with my friend," Deepak replied, smiling. "My phone was switched off, man. Was there anything important?"

"Of course, I talked to my boss about you and extra hours at the gas station." David had started working at a gas station after leaving the balloon animal job.

"What did he say?" Deepak looked up, his eyes widened and nostrils flared wide open.

"He said he'd give you a job at the gas station. You can start tomorrow," David looked pleased with himself. "You can go to work with me in the morning, and I'll teach you how to close up." Deepak was looking for a part time gas station job because he had heard that they would pay a bit more than the pay at restaurants or subway.

"Wow, really?" In Deepak's excitement, he hugged David. "Thank you. Thank you so much." Deepak was happy for all the success being lined up. The American dream dawned on him again.

He went to bed.

Chapter 26: Mud and Stars

Deepak started working at the gas station two days a week during the days he did not have to go to Succulent Sandwiches. There were miscellaneous items displayed on the gas station's counter: different kinds of cigarettes with different flavors, Black and Mild's in different colors and sizes, candies, Lotto, gum, and so on.

It took him a while to memorize the different items in the showcases. He did, however, remember the names of various cigarette brands quickly with the help of David. He worked at the register and learned how to ring up purchases. This was not too difficult for him because he had already spent time working at a register at Succulent Sandwiches. When Deepak wasn't at the register, he was collecting the trash outside by the pumps and cleaning the floor.

David taught him everything he needed to know. After several days of training, Deepak was ready to close the store on his own at night. It felt good to be given this level of trust and responsibility.

One day, he closed the store and left. The roads were almost deserted by time he got out. It was late, but he didn't have far to walk. He shoved his hands in his pockets and started heading back to the apartment. The faint sound of footsteps behind him caused Deepak to turn around. He could see two distinct shadows following him. There was a hammering in his chest, and Deepak realized it was his heartbeat.

No sooner had he thought those words then four arms grabbed him. The cold, sharp blade on his throat told him he was not dreaming. He had not realized that he had closed his eyes, but when he opened them he saw two young men in their early 20s, one white and the other a light skinned black guy. One look at their glazed eyes told Deepak that these men were high as kites.

"Where is your money? Give me money," they said. They both began to push Deepak against a nearby wall.

"I don't have any money," Deepak stammered. He grasped the straps of his backpack until his knuckles blanched white. Deepak thought of kicking their balls and running away from them, but he hesitated. They didn't have a gun so Deepak thought he could make it.

Using all the strength he could muster, Deepak swung his whole body around and hit the guy that held the knife with his backpack. As that man fell, Deepak lashed out with a leg and caught the other guy's balls with a hard kick. At that moment, a car honked as it passed them, startling the rest of the men. Without looking back, Deepak darted across the road and ran. He ran all the way home and pushed through the front door.

"Why are you so late today?" David asked.

"I was robbed," Deepak stammered. His voice sounded like it was getting lost inside his throat.

"What the hell are you talking about?" David shouted, surprised.

His voice grew weak, and the sound turned into staccato-like breathing. "I barely escaped with my life," Deepak said, drained of emotion. Even if it was a day of cold months, Deepak was sweating.

"How did it happen?"

Deepak was not in a mood to explain anything in detail. "I can't think about anything at this moment," He dropped to his knees on the floor. "Please do not ask me."

When every time something good happens to me, it is plagued by something bad immediately afterward, Deepak threw his fist in the air. He lay in a crumpled fetal position. It was as if someone had kicked him and was still kicking him. His body shuddered. Only groans and stifled sobs escaped his mouth.

"Deepak, Deepak, tell me what happened," David continued.

He did not answer. He rushed to the bedroom. David was scared for his friend, and after some hesitation, he moved into the doorway of the bedroom.

"What happened? Please tell me," David begged. "They tried to rob me!"

"Who robbed you? What happened?" he insisted.

"Two men cornered me and held a knife to my throat. I was helpless. I fought them back and ran."

"Did they take any money?"

"Why are you asking me these stupid questions? I'm tired of answering your questions. Are you a cop? Does it matter?"

"I'm just asking, brother."

"Shut the fuck up. Just stop!" This was the fifth time he was using the word "fuck."

"I understand you, my friend. Why are you so mad?" David spoke calmly.

"Fuck you," he yelled, hitting the wall with his fist hard. "Fuck you. I don't care if you understand. I can't stay in this fucking land. Every penny I earn, they try to take it away from me. American dream is going to kill me!" He screamed as if he had been stabbed. Tears streamed down his face.

"Don't say that," David pleaded.

Deepak crumbled to the floor and sobbed. David realized there was no consoling him and let him release his anger and frustration. After a while, Deepak got up from the corner of the room and approached with his head bowed, tears still falling. "Sorry. My mind was messed up just now."

"It's okay, man. I understand."

"Let's go outside and smoke," Deepak begged, walking up and down the living room floor. They went out on the patio, and David lit a cigarette for each of them.

"I need to go back home, David," Deepak sounded empty, inhaling the first puff and exhaling it. But what to say to Melissa he was not sure. He would not want to tell all these things to Melissa. He wanted to prove that he was a strong man and ready to make his American dream come true.

"Don't make a quick decision like that," David spoke gently.

Deepak took a deep breath and said, "I don't know. I'm in a dilemma. I cannot live in fear for my life every time I go to work. I might die at gun point tomorrow. If I die, my parents will die in wailing and pain"

"This is the land of opportunity. We have to struggle and struggle to get ahead."

"Fuck that! What kind of land of opportunity, the struggle are you talking about? This country is rich outside, but it has lots of depravity inside. You know, two old guys came to the gas station today and asked for money to buy food. I sympathized with them. They were very old, and they didn't have money. I took some money from the register and gave it to them. Even if my country is poor, their kids care for old people. They do not have to beg for food in their old age. If you are sick, you will die here without the right amount of money. That's not a problem in my country," Deepak said, holding the cigarette that was slowly turning into ashes.

"I hear what you're saying. I feel it. But you're still young, and you've got many things to do. Don't hesitate facing the challenge." David said, smoking the cigarette and puffing the smoke out. "Look at me." The smoke wandered in ringlets.

A chilling wind started blowing outside.

"Let's go inside, Deepak, and talk," David said, hurling the cigarette butt on the ground. "It is freezing out here."

"Let me stay here a little bit," Deepak smiled

173

wryly. "Hey, what will happen when I go to work tomorrow? What happens if the same guys come back and shoot me to death? My parents would be devastated. Who will pay my loans back home? Who will pay my mother's medical bills?" Deepak smoked deeply and puffed it out until it disappeared.

"Don't think that way," David said, hugging himself in cold.

"I don't know," he said throwing the filter away, and they both went inside.

Deepak could not sleep that night. He kept taking long breaths and pacing around the living room. "I must go home. I must go home," he murmured.

It was four in the morning by the time he went to bed. Deepak saw David was already in a deep sleep with his face down on the floor. They had no real beds, only three mattresses on the floor where each man slept.

Deepak changed his mind and went outside to smoke another cigarette. He watched the smoke swirling off into the sky and tried to calm his mind. He thought of his family. Just then, his phone rang. He picked up his cell phone and held it to his ear.

"Hello," Deepak said softly.

"This is your father. How are you?" His voice sounded shaken.

"I'm good, *Buba*," Deepak lied. "How are you?"

"We have something very sad to tell you."

"What?" Deepak asked, his heart hammering again in his chest.

"We are mourning."

"What are you talking about, *Buwa*? Please, tell me."

"Your grandmother passed away today."

Deepak went numb with grief. He had not imagined that she would pass so soon. She was old and puckered, but she was healthy and hearty. Even in her late 90s, her body was tall and straight, she didn't need

174

a cane to help her walk. Deepak thought she would live at least another ten years or longer. She always told him that it was her dream to attend his wedding ceremony before she died.

"Don't eat salty food for 13 days and don't eat any meat," his father told him before he hung up the phone. From earliest childhood, Deepak had known that Hindus would not eat salty food for thirteen days when a family member had died, and that the sons and close family members who cremated the body were supposed to wear white clothes for 45 days.

"I won't *buwa*," Deepak said. His thoughts drifted.

His grandmother used to call America: *Gai Khane Desh*, which meant the country where people eat beef. She was a very dogmatic Hindu and would not let others touch the food she cooked. If someone touched her food, she would throw it away. She cooked for herself and wouldn't eat from anyone else. She would wash not only her hands, but also between her legs every time she urinated. When she entered the bathroom, in fact, she brought her own clean bucket of water.

She always had a religious story to tell even if the listener was reluctant to hear it. If she found they were uninterested in her story, she would say, "It was worthless to talk to you." She never liked staying with her sons, even in her old age, because her sons ate meat unlike her. She chose to live in a dorm adjoining a temple. Many dogmatic Hindus, like his grandmother, preferred to live near temples. Families made small living quarters with the purpose of providing people like her with food and shelter. "Make me a temple-like house. I will live there," she used to say.

"Nobody can resist death," Deepak spoke to himself. "Grandma, I will come to meet you one day." Deepak murmured, wiping the tears that had gathered in the corners of his eyes. He knew death was inevitable, and he could not live in fear of it. He could only live to the best of his ability now, with courage.

"May your soul rest in heaven!" Deepak Whispered.

Chapter 27: Beginning Again

Deepak decided not to go to the gas station and just to continue working at Succulent Sandwiches. The news of his grandmother's passing had galvanized him. He felt bloodied, but he knew he was not beaten. "Be the best person, my grandson," she had said. "I want you to be a fighter in life." Deepak did not want to let her down by returning to Nepal like a dog with his tail between his legs. "I am going to stay here and fight for my dreams," Deepak murmured.

It was Deepak's last semester. Parked cars were clad with a thin layer of snow. Branches of trees hung low, bowing toward the ground, which was wet with the dripping morning dew and snow. Deepak went to the bus station to get a ride to work. The wind blew cold, and he hugged himself tightly, as though he was stopping his finger from bleeding. The cold felt like a knife, almost unbearable.

After Deepak waited for half an hour, a bus stopped and a gaggle of people, including him, got on. The bus was warm, and slowly life began to return to his frozen nose and fingers. His toes took their time to thaw. Deepak's teeth were chattering, but they eventually stopped. When he got to work in the mall, Rita was busy making bread, and Vikas was working at the register.

"Hello, *Bhaisaeb*. What's up?" Vikas questioned. He was standing at the register.

"Not much," Deepak said. Rita smiled at Deepak.

Deepak changed into his Succulent Sandwiches uniform and started sweeping the floors in his area. He wanted to put the incident of his night job as far away as possible from his memory. He put ice in the icebox and washed all the dishes Rita had left in the sink for him. He put bread in the oven and got cookies ready for baking. He made sweet and unsweetened tea. He cleaned the counters with a damp rag. He greeted customers and rang up their orders quickly.

"You have a good day, sir," Deepak said, handing a customer his receipt.

"Good job!" Vikas beamed after the customer had left. "You make me very happy, boss." Vikas teased.

"Thank you," Deepak said, leaving the register. "Oh, we're running out of chips. Let me fill them."

"Boss, I will do that," Vikas said, keeping up the charade, clearly in a good mood. "You have already done so much."

Another customer approached, a man in his early 20s. He had tattooed his arms and chest with nude pictures of young women in the way a Hindu *fakir* anoints his body with ash. He had pierced his tongue, ears, nose, lips, cheeks, chin, and eyebrows, which made him look like the ten-headed *Roundhe*, an evil character in Hindu mythology. His girlfriend had similar markings, with a pierced navel, which was tattooed underneath it.

"*Shit,*" Deepak whispered nodding his head in disapproval.

When the customers left, Rita approached Deepak and scoffed, "If my kids looked like that, I would slap them to death."

"But what can you do in this country?" Deepak asked her, laughing and scrubbing the front of microwave. "We cannot tell them do this or that after they turn eighteen."

"That's right," Rita agreed. "But our children won't do that."

"You never know," Deepak added. "If you scold them, they might call the cops. What can you do? This is America. They think that they are free to do what they like when they turn eighteen."

Rita remained quiet and started doing the fill up. Deepak just continued murmuring picturing their nipples and navels being pierced and boobs, bellies, and butts being tattooed, not even being able to wrap his head around it. A long line of customer was already waiting for sandwiches.

Chapter 28: Rebellious love

When Deepak arrived at campus, Melissa was already there standing by the classroom door as though she was waiting for him. Today was the last day of the semester. In other words, it was the last day of the program. Deepak was excited about completing the program soon and walking in his graduation. He looked deeply into Melissa's face. Her face seemed to glow when he approached and her smile reached her eyes.

"Hi," she said, smiling.

"Hi" he said, smiling back.

"Should we go inside?"

"Yes," Deepak said. Melissa was wearing a blue top, blue denim jeans, and a blue overcoat that perfectly matched her blue eyes. Her lips were glossy. She had her hair cut, a different look for Deepak.

The professor arrived, opened the door, switched on the lights. The students clambered in after her, falling into familiar seats and digging into their backpacks to take out their exercise books with the final project assignments they were going to turn in.

After a few hours, the class was over.

Melissa looked at Deepak and he felt warmth bubble up inside of him. Melissa walked out before him and waited outside. Together, they strolled to the parking lot.

"Deepak, my mom and my sister are visiting me today. I want to introduce you to them. Do you want to come over?" Melissa said, opening the door of her car.

"Sure," Deepak responded. The elation Deepak felt lit up his eyes as he eagerly climbed into her car. Melissa played music and lowered the volume until it hummed. Deepak caressed her back gently. When they arrived at the apartment, her mother and sister were watching television. They flicked it off quickly when they saw that they had company.

"Hello, my name is Rena," Melissa's mother said, shaking Deepak's hand as she stood to greet him. She was a few inches taller than her daughter and had shoulder-length dark brown hair that complemented her tanned skin. Her eyes were a piercing, icy blue, the only thing that really resembled her daughter. The blue silk dress she wore made her eyes sparkle. *I see, where her likes of blue dress was coming from*, Deepak thought silently.

"I'm Deepak. Nice to meet you," Deepak said extending his hand.

"Nice to meet you," she said, showing him the couch. "Please, have a seat."

"Thank you," he said taking a seat on the edge of the couch.

"May I make you some coffee?" Rena said, gesturing to Melissa.

"I'm okay. Thank you," he said. Back in Nepal, they would have forced him to drink the coffee. There, it would be considered a sign of respect to force a guest to eat something. In America, it was rude to insist. Deepak knew that.

"She sings opera very beautifully," Melissa said, pointing to her sister. "Do you like opera Deepak?

"Yes I like it, but I never understood what they were saying."

"Sing a song for him, please," Rena said to her daughter.

"What's your name?" Deepak asked, looking directly at the younger girl's face.

"Marina," she blushed. She was blonde like Melissa. Her eyes were the same color as her mother. She had long legs that were encased in a white flowing skirt, patterned with dainty embroidery.

"Please sing one for him," Melissa and her mother persisted. Marina, stood up, took a deep breath, stared out in front of her, and sang:

L'amour est un oiseau rebelle
Que nul ne peut apprivoiser,
Et c'est bien in vain qu'on l'appelle
S'il lui convient de refuser.

Melissa translated the song for Deepak.

"Love is a rebellious bird
That nothing can tame,
And it is in vain to be called
If he should refuse."

He enjoyed the song once Melissa translated it to him.

"Thank you, Marina," Deepak said. The whole family seemed intent on pleasing him.

"You're welcome," Marina responded, her visage blushed.

Melissa explained that the song was from an opera by Bizet called Carmen, which told the story of a wild girl who fell in love with a man who tried to tame her and eventually killed her. The story was sad, but the song was so lively that Deepak made a mental note to find out more about the opera.

"Wonderful family!" Deepak said. He felt very proud to be in love with Melissa, who saw him as someone worthy of her love, not to be pitied or mocked. They sat in the living room and talked more about Deepak's background and plans after graduation. He learned that Melissa looked more like her father's Irish family, but she definitely had the sweet, loving nature of her mother, who would, at times, mention his "intentions." Melissa's father was divorced a year ago, Melissa had told him. *How can people get divorced in such a sweet and beautiful family?*, Deepak thought. *Perhaps they could not look for what they had in common.*

After an hour or so of conversation, Deepak asked

for permission to leave.

Melissa dropped him off at his apartment and left him with her kiss. "I love you," she whispered.

Deepak found himself humming the song from the opera all night. He couldn't sleep when thoughts of Melissa ran around in his head. Thoughts of Melissa, her family, their hospitality, and the rebellious bird that could not be tamed stayed with him until daybreak.

Chapter 29: Sunrise or sunset

The day that, he thought, would never come soon enough had arrived almost without warning. His graduation was tomorrow. After the first semester of his arrival in the US, Deepak's time flew by despite some hurdles and hardships. Melissa's entry in his life eased him.

It was his last day at Succulent Sandwiches.

"You are a different person now, *bhai*," Rita said to Deepak.

"Why?" Deepak wondered. "How, *didi?*"

"I do not see any regret and the feeling of humiliation in your face," Rita said, looking at him. "You seem to be enjoying the work no matter what. You look happy at the work you do."

"Thank you, *didi*," Deepak said with a smile on his face. "I learned that we all should respect jobs that help reach our goal. This job has really taught me who I am and where I am now. No work is smaller or bigger. Work is work. So, thanks to you, thanks to Vikas for teaching me the lesson."

"You are welcome," Rita said. "That's very good. Let me wash the remaining dishes."

"I will wash them, *didi*," Deepak said. "You take the customer."

"No, no you do it. I will wash them," she insisted. "Today is your last day at work anyway."

Rita washed dishes in the back, and he could hear them clinking and clanging. Vikas came in saying, "Good morning," and opened the register.

"Boss, exactly when do you graduate?" Vikas asked playfully. He had started calling Deepak "boss" as a joke, but it had turned into a friendly sign of respect. Vikas was certainly pleased with the changes he saw in Deepak.

"Tomorrow," Deepak said.

"Oh, wow, congratulations! What's your plan after that?"

"I'm going to go to New Hampshire. My closest friend lives there with his wife. He has also supported me financially. Perhaps I will find a job there and live in his area. I have to make some money to pay the debt I owe people, you know."

"When you leave, we'll miss you here," Vikas said, looking at Deepak who was now filling up the ice-box.

"I wish I could stay, but I need to go. I have to find a job that has something to do with my qualifications," Deepak said, scooping the ice and putting it in a bucket

"Marry a white girl and get a green card first," Vikas suggested jokingly.

Deepak laughed, but he pictured getting married to Melissa and living the American dream. He smiled to himself.

"It's good you'll be graduating, but it is sad to see you leave," Vikas added, sounding as if he meant it.

"I thank you, Vikas. Succulent Sandwiches taught me to be the master of my own work and taught me to work hard."

"At least your hard days are almost behind you," Rita chimed in, her voice betrayed a measure of real sadness.

The day went by quickly and before he knew it, he was saying good bye to a job that had challenged him, making him cry in frustration. Still, it had taught him so much.

"Good luck, Deepak," Rita and Vikas both hugged him as he stood waiting to leave.

"Don't forget to call," Rita chided.

"How can I forget, my sister?" Deepak said.

Vikas took a $100 bill from the register and gave

185

it to him. "Deepak, take this from me. You helped me a lot. Thank you so much."

"No, no, thank you," Deepak said, trying to avoid the money. "You do not need to give me that."

"Please, take it. Think of it as a graduation present." Vikas shoved the money in his shirt's pocket and walked off.

Deepak hugged Rita again and walked out of Succulent Sandwiches with his head held high.

Outside the store, he inhaled deeply as if smelling fresh air for the first time.

When Deepak arrived at the apartment, David was packing things and putting them in a luggage.

"Why are you packing up your clothes, David?" Deepak asked

"I am leaving the country," David said.

"What?" Deepak said with his jaw lowered. 'Why? You didn't even mention that to me?"

"My mom is very sick. I gotta go. I don't know if I'll come back," David said folding his clothes and putting them in the luggage one by one.

"What the heck are you talking about, man?" Deepak fumed. "People die to come to America and you are already here. Isn't that what you told me? Look at me, I wanted to return home after I got mugged, but I stayed after you encouraged me." Currently Deepak had a lot of hopes to look for—graduation, and his girl friend Melissa.

"What do I have in this country? I have no *real* job, I have no big money, and my mom is sick back home," David snorted back at him. "Now you are going to graduate. Now you have a girlfriend. Your days are getting better. You live here. I don't," David said, without looking at Deepak and just concentrating on packing his clothes.

"Are you serious?" Deepak balked at the girlfriend

jab because David knew how long it took for him and Melissa to even become official. His longtime fantasy had only recently become a reality.

"There is nothing wrong in my country," David said. "It was all in my bullshit mind to chase some American dream."

"What about all the things you told me when I wanted to leave?"

"I told you those things because I had to help you. I'm your friend, aren't I? It's easier said than done. Many of my friends couldn't get a job worth their qualifications and have already returned home. I don't want to stay here and work at a gas station for the rest of my life. I want to live a meaningful life. You can work hard and stay here, but I cannot."

"David, it will get better," Deepak said approaching him and patting his back.

"I don't need any advice. I'm tired, and I've thought about this for a while. I'm leaving." He said removing his hand forcefully. Deepak knew David was frustrated. He did not argue with him and followed him into the kitchen.

"Sorry, man," David said. "I don't mean to hurt you. You know I'm frustrated. I don't want to stay in this country. I think I can do much better if I go back to my own country."

He hugged Deepak, who started to cry, already missing his friend.

"We will be in touch." David left.

Deepak called Melissa and then went to see her—it was just a fifteen minute walk.

"I will come pick you up," she said.

"No worries, I will be right there," he said.

She welcomed him with a tight hug and long kiss. As he pulled away from her, she held his hand and looked into his eyes, her forehead furrowing in confusion.

"Are you okay?" Melissa said.

He told her about David and the mugging incident. Deepak exhaled deeply, as if a heavy weight had been lifted from his shoulders.

While he spoke, Melissa rubbed his back, and they snuggled closer. He showered her face with tiny kisses. "I love you, Melissa."

"I love you, too," Melissa said passionately.

"Darling, I wanna marry you," Deepak proposed out of nowhere. She remained silent.

"We can go to New Hampshire and live together, find a job, and get married," Deepak kept talking sitting on a couch and playing with her hair even though he did not hear a single word from her.

In Nepal, being in a relationship for a month or two was more than enough time to propose, and they had known each other for a lot longer than that.

He ran his fingers though her hair. She had cut it, and it was so short now that Deepak could feel the softness of her scalp.

"You cut your hair," he said, "so now I can't play with it. Don't cut your hair anymore, okay?"

She remained silent as Deepak gazed into her eyes. Finally she asked, "How many kids would you like to have?"

"Not more than two," Deepak said looking into her eyes.

"What about four?" Melissa asked.

"I can handle four as long as we could take care of them all," Deepak said with a smile.

"If you have four kids and raise them in a good environment, there will be four more wonderful people in the world instead of just two," she said returning the smile.

"Sounds logical," Deepak laughed and held her tighter.

"I have another question for you," Melissa said.

"What's that?"

"Suppose your wife wakes up and all of a sudden tells you that she is not going to work anymore, what would you do?"

"I would tell her to do what makes her happy," he said and changed the subject. "By the way, tomorrow is my graduation. You'll be there, right?"

Melissa had not finished with her final project and that would take her next semester to graduate even if she was done with all the courses that needed to be taken in person. Deepak had already submitted his thesis titled "Running from the Dreamland" and his committee had accepted it so he was ready for graduation tomorrow.

"Yes," she said. "I'll definitely be there. You are my love. What are you talking about?"

"I can't wait to see you tomorrow," Deepak said and kissed her.

She dropped him off at his apartment. "Love you," he said and she said.

Chapter 30: Melissa's Letter

Deepak looks around. Nobody is there. All the graduated students are gone. Some of them who were taking selfies earlier are no more. Only street lights and the lights on the university's premises are on. Trees, buildings, and empty ground welcome him. The hall in front of him where they marched this afternoon is empty. Melissa is not around. He becomes sure Melissa will, for sure, not come. He looks at his phone and the time is 9 P.M. He realizes he spent two, three hours sitting there and reminiscing about his two years in America.

He slowly gets up, instead of going to Melissa's apartment, he decides to go to his own apartment with a feeling of dejavu; he checks his email. Melissa has sent him a message.

Deepak,

I had a lot of things going on in my mind that I was unable to tell you when you were in front of me. I am not a sentimental person, so I don't cry. I don't like to share everything I feel, and poetry is usually my only outlet. Today, I would like to tell you how I really feel. I was born in a Catholic family, and I want my kids raised in a Catholic family. I appreciate that you're open and respect all religions, and that you have a single concept of God. But for me, Jesus is the only God, and that may not be an issue with us now, but your family would not go for it. You want us to move and go around your family and friends who would reject my beliefs. That's too much to ask.

Furthermore, you cannot order me to do this or that. I can do whatever I like. If I want to have my hair cut or dance a tango in the street, I am going to do that. I am an American girl, and you should understand where I'm coming from. I cannot move immediately

190

with you wherever you want to go. I have plans too, and you never considered them or even asked. My life can't be all about making you happy, which I've tried to do so far. We always talk about your disappointments and dreams, but never mine.

I now realize that love is not enough, and we are just not right for each other. Still, I wish you all the best,
Melissa

Reading the message, Deepak feels dumfounded. He cannot believe what he is reading. With Melissa, he has a little bit of happiness, but like everything else, it vanishes without warning. The American dream becomes a distant memory right away.

He escapes the apartment to take a walk, not sure where he is going. He lights a cigarette and puffs furiously as he walks and finds himself in the town center. In a strip mall, the green lights of an Irish shamrock welcome him to *O'Riley's Pub.* He orders some whiskey and immediately starts drinking.

"Hey, Deepak." Deepak glances up with surprise to see Vanessa sitting beside him. She looks as pretty as ever; he almost pinches himself to see if she is real.

"What are you doing here?" she asks as she hugs him. Her breasts push against his chest with her embrace, and her breath smells Margareta.

"This is the celebration of my graduation, Vanessa," although he smiles, there are tears in his eyes. "I graduated today, but none of my friends were there. So, here I am by myself." He has to shout above the noise of the other revelers.

"Wow, congratulations, Deepak," Vanessa calls back, looking very happy for him. "Here we are to celebrate then," Vanesa opens her arms as if she is welcoming Deepak into her embrace, pointing to a guy next to her, and says, "This is Deepak, my former roommate. He graduated today. Deepak, this is my boyfriend, Mike." Mike looks slimmer and taller than

Lucas.

Deepak reaches over and shakes hands with him. "Nice to meet you."

"Nice to meet you," Mike replies. "Congrats, bro."

"Thank you."

A few more rounds of drinks later, Vanessa and Mike offer to drop him off at his apartment. He gladly accepts, knowing that he is drunk.

"Enjoy living as a graduate now in America, *Chico*," Vanessa calls out as she closes the car door.

"Thank you, Vanessa," he mumbles.

Deepak knows it is not a good idea to go to Melissa's apartment so early, but he has to speak with her. He is somewhat drunk and thinks to go to Melissa's apartment.

He knocks on the door of her apartment. Her lights are on, so he knows she is up. In his drunken stupor, he calls out her name. The door opens and Melissa stares at him, her eyes narrowed.

"Deepak, I thought I made myself clear in the email. Why are you here?"

"I just need to tell you about my change of plans," he says almost slurring in an unusually boisterous tone.

"Listen, you had better come in. Half the neighbors have probably heard you." She opens the door, and he shuffles in, dejected.

"Melissa, I know what you said in your email, but that can't be it. We've known each other for far too long." He collapses onto her sofa.

"Deepak, you're a good man, but we're too different; life with you wouldn't work." She sits in a chair opposite him, dressed in a long turquoise dressing gown that swept the floor, her delicate hands played nervously with her short-cropped hair. Her toenails are painted black.

"Melissa, Melissa, I know I'm a little drunk, and I know I've been a fool, but are we really that different?"

He is holding his head in his hands and swaying slightly. He continues, "If we concentrate on our differences, then we will always drift apart, but what about the things that we have in common?" He feels like crying, and a year ago, he would have been in tears, but now he knows this is not the time.

"Melissa, how long have we known each other? Before you met me, did you know anyone else from my part of the world?" He continues.

She merely listens with tears in her eyes, allowing him to speak. "My darling, think of the things that you have taught me and that you might have learned from me. I'm not certain about anything now, Melissa. I thought I knew everything and where I wanted to be in the world, what I wanted to do. The only thing that I'm certain of is that I love you. I can't believe it myself, but when you said that you did not want to see me, nothing else seemed to matter. I don't care about what you wrote—I mean, I respect it—but your words are not the reality that we have lived this past year, my darling."

Sighing, she sits back in her chair. "Deepak, look at me," she says. He lifts his head from his hands and stares at her. "I know what you say is what you feel in your heart, and I know that it was unkind of me to write you instead of saying it to you face to face. But I knew that if I saw you, I might change my mind. I'm sorry, but right now, I'm not sure of what I want."

Tears roll down Melissa's face, but she remains silent. He gets up from the sofa and she from her chair. They hug each other, and he leaves and gets back in his apartment and falls asleep as whiskey in his body makes him tired and perhaps forgetful.

Epilogue: Running from the Dreamland

The next morning, wet weather announces itself by pounding on the cars parked in the apartment complex. Deepak looks through the horizontal white plastic blinds that hang over the window. The water slithers down the windowpane and blurs the scene outside. His body aches. Slowly he stretches over the side of the bed and pulls the laptop onto his lap. It weighs a ton. Deepak opens it and inches his way through all the emails in his inbox. All of them are from friends in Nepal, asking how he is doing and wishing him the best. He replies to them all with three words, "I miss you!"

He checks all the emails. First, he reads a message his sister sent him. Reading his sister's email, Deepak knows that his parents are worried about him and want to know how he is doing. He writes her back:

Everything is good and fine. I'm doing great. Don't worry about me. I just graduated. Life here is wonderful. My friends are great here, they look after me, and my roommates are very friendly.

Love, Deepak

Deepak does not want to let them know how lonely he is feeling without his family and friends. The thought of his parents knowing the full truth of his situation makes him shudder. He wants them to live peacefully in the knowledge that their son is doing well in the United States. He wants them to hold their heads up high amongst family and friends.

After reading the email, Deepak feels even lonelier. He has nothing in his mind but the absence of his relatives and friends, and the happiness he'd shared with them. To return to his home country would be the last resort. Once again, he reflects on his aspirations.

Deepak leaves the laptop on the side, tosses, and turns on his bed. Suddenly, his stomach is attacked by a spasm of pain that radiates around his navel. He wails like a kicked animal; his breathing becomes short and shallow. Adjusting himself in bed, he finds that the sheet is wet with perspiration. The joints in his body seems to rebel at the same moment, and he is gripped with intense weariness. Scratching his head, his fingers find a hard, foreign growth near his earlobe and he tugs at it, only to find it was merely a piece of dry skin. A vacant laugh escapes his lips and a dry mouth drives him from his bed to the refrigerator.

He brings back a bottle of water to his bed and sits on the edge, he gulps the bottle's water until it is empty and then throws the empty container by the bed and lies back down.

"I cannot live in America like this. I have to go back to my country, and contribute to her in any way I can. If we all leave our motherland for developed countries, who will care for her? I have to go back to my country and change the system. I have to try to do something that will help my country develop," He mumbles, lying on his back with his hands folded and legs extended.

Deepak gets up from the bed with aching limbs and again peers out through the window blinds. It is still raining. Water is falling off the leaves of the trees. The ground is wet, and in some places puddles appear.

Leaving his place of refuge, Deepak goes to the bathroom. The bathroom is a dingy cream color, he never realized. The cupboards are once white, but are now chipped and the paint is flaking off the corners. A curtain separates the toilet from the bath, decorates with seashells and seahorses.

He recalls the great Nepali poet, Laxmi Prasad Devkota, who wrote an essay, *"Ke Nepal Sanu chha,"* meaning "Is Nepal a Small Country?" A line of the

195

essay floats into his memory: *though the human eyeballs are small, they are precise and important, and so is Nepal.*

He pictures the fields of mustard and the families of ferret-badgers stealing through the rows of yellow flowers. The green paddy fields and the mounds of rice shaped like little huts, drying in the sun come to mind. His father is still tilling the rice fields, his back bends as he stoops to weed the tender plants, and his mother might be cooking *dhal* and rice. Deepak sees her on the rooftop with the large, circular tray, sifting the grains of rice, tossing them up into the air and separating the chaff from the grain. He also pictures her helping his father as he toils in the fields. Perhaps they manage to buy some more chickens. He visualizes the moment and feels emotion well up in his chest.

Deepak's mind is still racing. He pictures his whole family waiting for him with garlands in their hands at the tiny airport in their town. He sees himself sitting next to his mother and eating rice from stainless steel plates, neatly divided in sections: the largest part for the rice, and smaller sections for the curry and pickles. He sees himself in the kitchen, surrounded by his family as they mill around him. He pictures the girl who his parents had chosen for him.

"No more of this falling in love business," he mutters to himself. "Marriage and family will come like it does for everyone else back home." He sees himself opening a school and teaching English to children in Nepal. His dreams seem to have changed. He is taking the path of those people who saw no real potential in him. "I am what I am," he murmurs.

Deepak refuses to become Ganesh, and he realizes that David is right about this fleeting pursuit. He makes his mind up to go home to begin a new life. He does not want to live the American dream. He is going home because that is where he wants and needs to be. These thoughts circle in his brain. His fallible memory travels back to his childhood life at school and the countryside and village.

A scrawny kid, Deepak is sitting poolside behind his high school throwing pebbles in the pool and watching the ripples they produced. Friends come and invite him to join their game of hide and seek, but he declines, remaining transfixed on the water. The school bell rings. They all rush toward the building where the teacher already entered the classroom. The teacher pulls their sideburns as a punishment for being late. As friends, they take delight in their mischievousness and enjoy being punished as a group. A beautiful girl, about his age, always kisses him before they leave school. On his way back home in the countryside, Deepak steals cucumbers from the neighbor's farm and gobbles them secretly, running away as the farm owner chases him and his friends.

In winter, old folks are outside in their courtyard basking in the sun while others are around the fire. In the rainy seasons, villagers till the earth and plant rice, and Deepak watches them or helps with their work. He walks around the farm with a radio swinging across his shoulder while listening to the song Gauradako Bazzaraima. In the harvest time, the villagers collect rice plants, and when they ripen, they bring them to the courtyard. The villagers are sweating but happy, some might say jubilant. His father drinks water from a mug, and his long neck reveals an Adam's apple that twists and turns as the water runs down his throat.

He plays with mud, making mud castles and wandering around half-naked, only wearing briefs. A beautiful girl is his imaginary play friend. Deepak kisses her cheek, and she is happy. He likes her. No, he loves her. As he sits, young women a lot older than him pass by. He loves watching their breasts, and they call him "bad boy" when they find his eyes fixed on their chests.

Deepak sighs and a longing engulfs him. He

cannot forget the place where his heart yearns to return. He wants to run from the dreamland – if only for a moment – to reclaim distinct details of his former life and love.

On the plane back home, he contemplates his village. *What a loving name the word "village" itself is! It becomes even more loving when the past and the memories come with it and the heart beats in it. At times, I question the dreams we desire to have while not knowing we are already living it. Is our dream a shiny car on a slippery road or a cold breeze blowing by the mountain's lap? Is it a furnished mansion or a simple house furnished with a natural scene outside? Is it the city of skyscrapers or the sight of the skyscraper like mountains? Is it the manmade lake or spring or the natural ones? Is it the cacophony of modernism or the meditation like a murmur of the running stream? Is it the food that stays in the freezer before reaching the kitchen or the one that directly goes from the farm to the kitchen? Is it the modern world in our sight or the snow clad mountains, greeneries, plants and the bubbles of the rain? Is it the trail jam of the traffic during a morning drive or a trail we make while walking and smelling the soil and vegetation? Is it the pain we experience not having time to communicate with friends and families back home or the pleasure we receive meeting them every mealtime? So you tell me what is your dream or your dreamland?*

Running from the Dreamland

 Tulasi Acharya was born in the South Asian country of Nepal. He completed his Master's degree in English in Tribhuvan University in Kathmandu. He also taught English and Journalism courses at colleges in Nepal. A prolific writer, Acharya published short stories, poems, and articles in Nepali journals, national newspapers and online. He moved to the United States in 2008 to pursue a Master's degree in creative writing. He holds a Ph.D. in Public Administration from Florida Atlantic University, USA. Originally from Nepal, Acharya has a Master's degree in Women's Studies and a degree in Professional Writing too. His research interests are disability, policy, gender and sexuality, marginalized narratives, critical theory, and post colonialism, including creative writing and translation.

Books from the author: *Running from the Dreamland; Sex, Gender, and Disability in Nepal: Marginalized Narratives and Policy Reform*

Printed in the USA
CPSIA information can be obtained
at www.ICGtesting.com
JSHW030346030124
54559JS00009B/182